# LIVES OF THE DOG-STRANGLERS

Simon Mason is the author of two previous novels: *The Great English Nude* (1990), which won a Betty Trask Award, and *Death of a Fantasist* (1994). He lives in Oxford.

ALSO BY SIMON MASON

*The Great English Nude*
*Death of a Fantasist*

Simon Mason

# LIVES OF THE
# DOG-STRANGLERS

VINTAGE

Published by Vintage 1999

2 4 6 8 10 9 7 5 3 1

First published in Great Britain in 1998 by
Jonathan Cape

Vintage
Random House, 20 Vauxhall Bridge Road,
London SW1V 2SA

Random House Australia (Pty) Limited
20 Alfred Street, Milsons Point, Sydney
New South Wales 2061, Australia

Random House New Zealand Limited
18 Poland Road, Glenfield, Auckland 10,
New Zealand

Random House South Africa (Pty) Limited
Endulini, 5A Jubilee Road, Parktown 2193,
South Africa

Random House UK Limited Reg. No. 954009

A CIP catalogue record for this book
is available from the British Library

ISBN 0 09 974991 2

Papers used by Random House UK Ltd are natural,
recyclable products made from wood grown in sustain-
able forests. The manufacturing processes conform to
the environmental regulations of the country of origin

Printed and bound in Norway by
AIT Trondheim AS, 1999

For my parents

'In nova fert animus mutatas dicere formas corpora'
'Of bodies changed to other forms I tell'

Ovid, *Metamorphoses*
Translated by A.D. Melville

Author's Note:

This book is written in the mode of farce.

# DINNER

It was October 1989, a month of rain after the
long tranquillity of an Indian summer, and we were
standing outside Jeremy's house on the Hill, watching
the clouds bully their way across the bruised sky. The
Hill is an area of upland suburbia two miles south
of the city with a view of the spires; it specialises
in emeritus professors, ex-police commissioners and
superannuated politicians.

The rain came swirling up the valley in inky
clouds: it had been violent that year, dead leaves and
branches falling from trees, sudden storms dropping
out of low, discoloured clouds and bolts of bright
sunlight shattering the floodwater. But Jeremy was
in love; it was, he said, his 'springtime'. Jeremy was
twenty-four years old and more than touched with
adolescence.

For half an hour he had been talking about romantic love. Jeremy likes to talk. He has a particular
manner, by turns tragic and flippant. It is the well-
known Oxford manner. In time he will become one
of the self-tormented, talking of the class of '83 and
following his college's progress in the Norrington
table. Jeremy was my oldest friend, but we were
not alike.

While he talked, his girlfriend, the unfortunate subject of his soliloquy, ran her fingers through her dark hair and rubbed one shoe against the other, and kept her face away from mine, as if we had met before and she were afraid of being recognised. Her waxed jacket hung open: underneath she was wearing a white blouse, impeccable navy skirt, navy nylons and high heel shoes, very muddy. She was one of those attractive, finely-bred, inappropriately dressed girls who seem to be a factor of the local weather, capable of dissolving at any moment into nothing.

'This is Rebecca,' Jeremy said at last.

She provocatively prolonged the examination of her shoes.

'Lost something?' I asked, and she looked up with a spoilt toss of her head. Her nose was sharp, her eyes grey, her mouth as perfect and prim as a seashell, and in her face I read her character. Whatever she was given she would always be dissatisfied, she would respond to affection with indifference, to supplications with scorn, and in the end would prove untrustworthy. I concluded that Jeremy's love affair was doomed.

Jeremy began to talk of dinner parties. 'The art of the dinner party is the first art of civilisation,' he said. 'If I give a dinner party I bring perfection to the mundane, order out of chaos, spring weather out of rainstorms. Do you see? Dinner parties conform to a higher, paradoxical reality. This is not 1989, the month is not October, it is not raining.' The Oxford manner is essentially mock-heroic, contrived with such irony and taken to such extremes that the frivolous becomes serious, and vice versa. Jeremy talked about the dinner party he would give to mark, to *celebrate* his love for Rebecca – and the more burlesque he became the more he wanted to be taken seriously.

'*Do* you see?'

I caught Rebecca's eye.

'How can I explain?' he said to me. 'You are my oldest friend, and you disbelieve everything I say. Let me be clear. I must employ specialised jargon. When I say dinner party what I mean is *statement*; what I mean is *happening*; I mean *witness, transfiguration.*'

He wasn't talking about size or grandeur. Jeremy's means were strictly limited. He was planning a dinner for no more than five or six people which would, through sheer force of imagination, be metaphorical, an ordinary moment lifted out of the ordinary, a huge hoax but implacably serious.

'Conventional life is banal but we will live with intensity,' he said.

Finally we went inside. Unlike Jeremy, Rebecca and I were not oblivious to a soaking.

Jeremy's address was the Lodge, the Hill. He rented a square cottage situated at the entrance to the grounds of a typically large house called Ambledene. His landlord, Emeritus Professor Sir Ernest Booth, was a violent intellectual who could be seen in the evening driving his ancient wife through the gardens on the way to their squalid swimming pool. Another peculiarity was that he treated Jeremy like a son. In his eyes, Jeremy could do no wrong.

The Lodge was cold in winter (when all the windows froze on the inside), suffocating in summer (ants infested it) and smelt, whatever the season, of unwashed carpet, not an unpleasant smell but as persistent and indefinable as an air of sadness. The kitchen was too grand, the living room too cramped, and the shabby, colonial furniture (*chaise longue*, drinks cabinet, magazine rack) had an air of dust-sheets about them. There were mirrors everywhere, tarnished and filthy: on the landing, in the dining room, on the stairs, on the kitchen door, in the entrance hall. It was as if a previous occupant had been making a study of his life composed of a disconnected string of banal images, like a fly-on-the-wall television documentary: here he is getting out of the bath, here he is dropping a packet of cereal, here he is tripping up the stairs. All the walls were harshly stippled with white textured paint and if you brushed your arm against them, you bled.

Since he had been in the Lodge Jeremy had broken up with five girlfriends, one after the other, and until he met Rebecca he openly referred to it as the House of Calamity. His romantic yearnings were intense, even pathological, and he had reached the stage where he could only express them farcically.

That wet afternoon Rebecca and I sat listening to Jeremy talk about the dinner party while rainwater dripped off a blocked drainpipe onto the windowsill,

4

and everything he said sounded like a prologue to a disaster.

The date of the dinner party was fixed for three weeks ahead, and in the intervening period I kept bumping into Jeremy in town. He was always 'convulsed in the throes of arrangements', and would talk of nothing else. His manner was noticeably more tragic than flippant. The first time I met him he was coming out of the public library where he had been trying to find books on Afghan cuisine. Like all obsessives, he wanted above all the part of the past to which he did not belong, in this case Rebecca's travels as a teenager.

'I'm in love,' he said. 'Look at that.' And he held out a perfectly still hand. 'It's torture,' he said. 'It's flux, delirium, ebullition.'

I observed that he was enjoying himself.

'I've changed,' he said. 'Love has changed me completely, I'm not the same person.'

He was wrong of course, he hadn't changed at all, he was exactly the same. Love doesn't alter; it exaggerates what is already there. It shows us ourselves in different modes. At bottom, I believe, we remain ourselves.

The next time I ran into him the physical effort of his idealism was apparent: he was pale and filled with an unnatural energy. Probably his hands, which he did not show me, were shaking. None of the delicatessens in any city or town in the Upper Thames Valley region stocked prosciutto d'oca, he told me.

Prosciutto d'oca is a kind of smoked goose breast which Rebecca had once eaten in Florence. He listed the delicatessens he had tried: there were twenty-three of them. He talked at length about Rebecca and her unremarkable, unattainable past as if demanding his rights.

The last time I saw him he did not see me, he was arguing with the owner of one of those expensive and useless shops in the covered market which specialise in houseware, in this case candles. He was explaining in a rude, pedantic voice that he wanted orchid-scented candles. 'No, not common hothouse orchids. Musk orchids. You will have heard of the Musk orchid, it is famous for not smelling of musk, it grows wild in the Chilterns. Wait, I've got one here.' He produced a broken flower. 'Smelling of that. That's what I want. As you see, the colour must be the palest yellow.' The shop owner said something. 'But don't you do commissions?' I heard Jeremy ask with violent incredulity. I quietly left the shop before he had a chance to see me. Love, you might say, is not my speciality – but I do know it can't be put together like a dinner party. The situation was clear. Jeremy was my oldest friend after all. I went home, got Rebecca's telephone number from another of Jeremy's friends, and called her.

I did not see Jeremy again before the night of the party. All that week the weather grew worse, building to a melodramatic crescendo. It was a bad omen. On the Saturday there was a storm which lasted all day. Having hoped in vain that the dinner would be cancelled, my mood was bitter and careless.

The evening was weirdly lit, a sodden sky flapping like laundry over the Hill as I drove up from Parkside where I lived. Reversing quickly along the winding, high-hedged driveway, past the House of Calamity, I parked against a laurel bush where I would almost but not quite obstruct the Emeritus Professor whom I disliked. Then I sat in the car smoking cigarettes, listening to the storm, feeling the car shake in the wind, gusts denting the wet hedges on both sides and raindrops bursting on the windscreen. At intervals the other guests arrived, pulled up on the verge outside the Lodge, and went in without seeing me. Through the haze of rain I glimpsed the forms of the Emeritus Professor and his wife struggling across the wind-swept lawn. Carelessness or rage kept me in my car for nearly an hour, then I got out and walked through the wind and rain to the hosue, my long coat swirling round me like a shadow disconnected and wild.

Rebecca answered the door, and we stood looking at each other. She was wearing a pencil skirt and an expensive thin pullover of the same navy blue, and her dark, well-groomed hair was pinned up. For a few moments, while the rain smacked my face and the wind flung my coat about behind me, she stood fixed and supercilious in that harsh white entrance hall, looking at me. Her skin was chalky pale and drawn, her lips parted slightly as if she were about to speak. Then, without a word, she turned and led me

7

into the house, every movement of her slow, poised walk showing that she knew how intently I watched her as I followed.

In the living room Jeremy was pouring drinks. There were shadows under his eyes and a tic in his cheek. His head jerked from side to side like a bird's. 'Late,' he said when he saw me. His voice was a falsetto. He appealed to the room with a sherry bottle. It was a Manzanilla Pasada, and I wondered how far he had travelled to get it. 'This is history, this is the book of recorded time, and in it you are marked down and will be forever remembered as late. Sherry or gin?'

'Whiskey,' I said. 'Irish, if you've got it.'

Already part drunk, he turned towards Rebecca, drink in hand, as if to propose a toast, but she had turned away.

As planned, the party was small, there were only three other guests, and although I knew them, they were not friends of mine. Jeremy's friends have seldom been friends of mine. Philippa is a publisher; she always wears black and her manner is matter-of-fact. Eleanor and Josh, a married couple, work for rival charities and like to argue in public. When I arrived they were arguing, and I knew they would be arguing when I left. Eleanor is the kind of woman whose beauty (large eyes, dimples, pointed chin) disappears as you listen to her, as if your eyesight is actually impaired by her tedious rage. Josh, the intellectual, smokes and, to goad her, murmurs to himself. His smooth, inexpressive face is as implacable as his manner. Their patience in these roles is limitless. I wondered if they had been invited by mistake or to fulfil a symbolic function. Either way it was obvious that the party was going to be worse than imagined. Lounging with my whiskey, and saying little, I kept an eye on Rebecca who sat primly on a high-backed chair with her legs crossed, listening to Josh and Eleanor. I was thinking of our telephone conversation.

I had expected her to have a telephone manner, and she did, a pert, snooty voice conjuring up just-so blouses and spectacles. I said, 'This is Jeremy's friend, we met the other week.'

'Jeremy has a number of friends,' she said in that snooty voice.

'We met on the Hill. It was raining.'

'It has been wet.'

I spoke very quietly, partly because I wanted to intimidate her, partly because I liked imagining her with the receiver pressed to her ear. I said, 'I've known a few bloodsuckers in my time. They're death. In the last five months Jeremy has been through five breakups. He can stand a sixth.'

There was a pause, I could hear the receiver coming away from her ear, and I thought she was going to hang up, but then I heard her say, 'I remember you now.'

'Break it off,' I said. 'Or I will. You're killing him.'

'Yes,' she said. 'You have a big nose and a bad tooth in the corner of your mouth. Your manner is overconfident.'

'Break it off.'

'And if I don't?'

There was a quiet hiss in the receiver as if she was quietly laughing. I thought of that prim, perfect mouth opening, her teeth and tongue.

I said, 'I'll tell Jeremy we're fucking. I'm his oldest friend. Even if he doesn't believe me, he won't believe you.'

'I suppose you think you're being original.'

'I don't believe in originality. Neither do you. You're number six.'

'Your trousers were the wrong colour,' she said. 'Your hands were too still, your eyes too shifty.' And then she rang off.

She sat on her high, hard chair with her legs crossed and her chin up, not saying anything, not even answering Jeremy who spoke to her every time he came in from the kitchen where he was struggling with the cooking and getting drunk. He must have known that all his efforts were wasted. I realised that I had not heard her say a single thing since I arrived. She sat apart from us all, nursing her air of dissatisfaction. Her telephone manner suited her, I decided, not because it was snooty but because it lacked pity.

Eventually we went into the cramped dining room

and sat in candlelight on shabby Edwardian chairs round a large oval table for which there was no proper room. I was in the corner where the piano and an oversized oak sideboard met at right angles, and without leaning back I could rest my elbows on both simultaneously. Jeremy had hired some expensive cutlery and glasses which were arranged in an elaborate display. It is Jeremy's habit to overdo things. There were finger bowls, little baskets for the wine and a silver cruet in the form of entwining swans. An over-large chandelier I had never noticed before hung obtrusively over it all: perhaps he had hired that as well. There were no curtains on the windows, and the black panes streamed with rain. It was an appalling scene. He had aimed at sublimity and arrived at farce.

The food was of that complexity which has no justification: there was an onion tart with quail-egg mayonnaise and home-baked tomato and olive ciabatta bread; an exotic mixed salad; some small, chilled fish rather like a sardine but according to Jeremy far less common; a lime and vodka sorbet; guinea-fowl rubbed with mint jelly; a regional version of zabaglione made with a strange near-brandy produced only by the hill people of Montenegro; a variety of cheeses, none celebrated; and astonishing fruit which even Jeremy had forgotten the names of. It was all rather badly cooked; the cheeses were too hard and the fruit too soft. Each course represented a part of Rebecca's past, a place she had been to or a person she had known or a period in her life; the meal unfolded in front of us like her biography, teasingly elucidated by Jeremy. The appropriations were, in a sense, savage, but they were also banal, and Rebecca didn't attempt to conceal her boredom. With each course a different wine was brought out – never anything usual but always Peruvian or English or Afghan – and with each wine Jeremy proposed a desperate, almost (as the meal went on) self-mocking toast, each time longer and less intelligible; and at each speech Rebecca looked away as if pretending that she were not there, or that Jeremy were not there. Although she sat next to him, she was distant; she was remote from us all in fact, as if the wavering halflights from the gross chandelier might really dissolve her and leave her chair empty. She was a kind of emptiness.

This was his statement, his happening, his witnessing and transfiguration.

Throughout the meal Eleanor and Josh continued to argue, which says something for their devotion. By the time coffee and liqueurs were served they had been arguing for over two hours, gradually growing louder and more domineering. Jeremy was too drunk to divert them; I couldn't be bothered. Philippa tried once, was ignored, and said hardly anything else for the rest of the evening. Rebecca, I noticed, seemed content to let them argue; she even took an interest – in so far as she took an interest in anything – and made the occasional comment as if to help the argument along.

The argument deepened and speeded up. It developed the eerie, random power of a litany.

Josh smoked quietly, talking to himself while Eleanor became hysterical. The origin, motives and structure of the argument were lost; what remained was its violence. All other attempts at conversation died away. Half an hour passed without anyone except Eleanor saying a word. By eleven o'clock we had stopped wondering if the argument would ruin the party; we wondered only what its outcome would be.

In my experience there is a point in every release of passion beyond which control is lost and an impersonal momentum takes over. With love, as with violence. When Eleanor, apparently oblivious to everyone but Josh, pushed over her chair, and began to shout meaningless and disconnected obscenities at him (spittle running down her pretty chin), we realised that she had passed that point.

Once, when I was a teenager on holiday in Rome, I saw a woman attack her lover with a stiletto shoe. I was drinking an aperitif in a café in a square when, with the operatic flair for which that city is famous, a man and woman appeared above me on a balcony, both dressed in white nightshirts; and while the man appealed to the crowd which quickly gathered below, the woman struck him repeatedly from behind with her shoe until blood stained his nightshirt red.

Eleanor took off her shoe and showed it to Josh. He must have understood at once because he began to talk rapidly; but of course it was too late, and she struck him suddenly on the head. His hands jerked up and squirmed for the shoe, missed it, and she swiped him across his face.

Philippa gave a little cry, backed herself against the sideboard and looked to me for help. But I was looking at Rebecca. I couldn't take my eyes off her. She was sitting forward in her seat, looking up at Eleanor, her face shining with pleasure.

Josh began to bleed, then cry. This made no impression whatever on Eleanor who beat him wildly, sweeping crockery and glasses off the table. Her technique was girlish, almost coquettish, but it was effective. Josh offered little resistance, staggering against the table and chairs, bleeding onto his shirt collar and sobbing, until finally she knocked him to the ground.

At this point Jeremy blundered in from the kitchen, drunk and disorientated, looking – naturally enough – as if he had just woken from a nightmare. He collided with Philippa who had belatedly leaped forward to restrain Eleanor, and they crashed awkwardly together onto the floor. Falling, Jeremy grabbed the table-cloth, and the table, an antique gate-leg, unexpectedly buckled and collapsed onto them. Josh and Eleanor continued to fight in the chaos. The cruet span up from nowhere and smashed a window, and as if this were a cue, the chandelier lurched down and broke on Josh's head. It was suddenly dark. He rose up and fell back down shouting onto the wreckage of the table. There was a pause, as if the room could do no more, the only sound the quiet rattle of many-voiced panting in the dark shadows, and then the piano suddenly sagged sideways with a boom and crushed Jeremy's outstretched foot. This was the last thing Rebecca and I saw as we watched from the doorway, taking care to avoid the debris. She turned to me and her face was radiant and exhausted.

'You couldn't have broken it off, you wouldn't know how,' she said. 'Men don't.'

We went out and found the storm had stopped, leaving an unearthly stillness. She walked ahead of me across the wet grass with a well-bred, prancing step, head up. There were calls from the house, but we didn't look back, we were lost in ourselves, lost perhaps in contemplation of the spent violence behind us and the promised violence ahead. When we got to the car, under the windscreen-wiper there was a melted handwritten note of complaint from the Emeritus Professor which I tore off and flung over the hedge, and in that gesture was all the satisfaction I wanted or needed.

All this was several years ago now. I have not seen Jeremy since, though for a time he used to leave messages on my answerphone. I hear that he is married and has moved down the hill into Parkside, the favourite suburb of new families. Soon he will have children. Parkside is very respectable, he'll like it there. It has the great advantage for him of having no other adolescents, only old people and young families – he will be unrivalled as the street juvenile.

I moved out long ago. It wasn't my style. It is a

place where people have no lives, where they plan their lives like dinner parties.

Rebecca stayed with me for three months, then left. I haven't seen her either, and I don't know why she went. She would say that men never know, and no doubt she would be right.

A word about those three months. They were not happy – but happiness has never much interested me, as Rebecca knew, with her intuition, when I telephoned her that time. I realise now that I phoned to congratulate her on Jeremy's destruction. We had only one secret to share, and we were soon bored by it. I imagine that love – or fidelity – demands more variety. I waited in vain to be shown myself in different modes.

What about Jeremy? If I were the sympathetic not the critical type I might wonder what he thinks about that night now. Does he remember it as vividly as he wanted to? Probably, if he ever thinks about it, he blames it all on the house, the House of Calamity. Of course he will never realise what a success it was. What an event, what a happening of a dinner party, fulfilling so completely and dazzlingly his notion of transfiguration.

# BONFIRE

Bonfire night is dreaded in Parkside Road. Behind the quiet, orderly facades of the houses nothing is quiet or orderly. The elderly people who have lived there since they were born take no pleasure in fireworks; they moan violently to each other and go to bed early with a night-cap. The new families who have moved in are at exactly the wrong time in their lives: they spend the evening in turmoil, running into bedrooms to explain to their wide-eyed toddlers why they need not be frightened, rocking their screaming babies, and shouting insults at their whining terriers who skulk around their feet and trip them up. Their patience wears thin and their dinners go cold. Long before the explosions have died away they have opened the good bottle of wine which they had been saving for the weekend and have begun the arguments which will last, like the smouldering bonfires in nearby back gardens, for the rest of the evening. At half past ten they lie exhausted in bed, angrily debating whose turn it is to change the baby. At midnight, when the fireworks have ended, they are kept awake by slight familiar noises: distant sirens, barking dogs, the last train to London going past with its long, pained sigh. Periodically the baby wakes for a feed, and in the dead silences in between they toss and turn, haunted by images of domestic discord and the shine of moonlight through the curtains, and do not fall asleep until two and three and four o'clock in the morning when their dreams will be lit with the shabby glow of rumoured conflagrations. The clear sky in the interval before dawn will be packed with stars, the damp air sharp with the smell of wood smoke, and the beginnings of a frost visible under the street lamps, but they will miss all this, falling asleep just before the transformation and waking two hours later in the grey light, with hangovers, guilty consciences and vile memories.

This year – it was 1992 – Dr Harris foresaw these things and determined to take precautions. As soon as he arrived home from the surgery he went into the kitchen and attempted to feed temazepam to their dog, Tom. Tom was a cairn terrier with a craggy aloof face and low-tension glaucoma. Dr Harris was, by his own admission, an irascible man whose abusive outbursts offended his wife and (his wife asserted) distressed and perhaps corrupted their son. But he believed in, and worked tirelessly for practical good; no general practitioner at the Parkside clinic was more bound by a sense of duty. At his own estimation he was an intense, overburdened parent, and believed this to be the common condition. The temazepam he smuggled into large handfuls of Good Boy Choc Drops. Tom ate the chocolates and left the pills on the hall carpet in a sticky mess, and later he was sick. By then Dr Harris was engaged in conversation with his two-year-old son, Huw. Huw was a nervous, stubborn boy.

'The fireworks tonight,' Dr Harris was saying, 'might make a little bang, because of the gunpowder in them. But I don't want you to be frightened.'

Huw was playing with the remains of a burst balloon on the kitchen floor.

'You see,' Dr Harris went on, 'when you know how something works you don't need to be frightened of it.'

Huw looked up, a shred of burst balloon skilfully fixed to his nose.

'Good,' Dr Harris said. 'Now upstairs for a bath.'

The balloon shred fell off Huw's nose and he said, 'Bugger!' loudly.

Dr Harris caught his wife's eye and went into the hall and soaped dog vomit off the carpet.

Upstairs, he worked in his tiny study at the back of the house. Whenever his bleeper went he came downstairs to make a telephone call, then climbed back to his work. After an hour or so, when his attention to a statistical analysis of a diabetes study group in Denmark was flagging, he had the insight that he lacked common sense. Clear principles, dogged persistence and a sense of honour did not prevent an emotional volatility leading him into situations in which his natural timidity and anger were soon exposed, and though he yearned for banality, his life was intense and fraught.

From the window of his study he could see the jumble of back gardens with their conservatory extensions, sheds and greenhouses, and the wet, grey roofs of houses in the next street arranged in a broken line like a makeshift barricade. Night obscured and knitted their roughly geometric shapes, and he was affected by the beauties of buildings which are built not for spectacle but for use. The storms of October had given way to tranquil damp and cold. His thoughts were not clear but he felt a sense of community, of family almost, in his corner of sky and garden, and, quite suddenly and unexpectedly, he thought that he had never loved anything so much.

The first rockets began to appear over the roofs, dusty red streaks blooming suddenly with sharp retorts into flower-like patterns of coloured lights. Shortly afterwards he heard Huw crying in his room, and a quarter of an hour later, when he could stand it no longer, he went along the landing into Huw's room, picked him out of bed, and carried him outside onto the patio. His actions were, he felt, gentle but firm. There was a moist wind blowing and the bituminous smell of smoke and gunpowder in the air.

'Shall we see if we can see some rockets?' Dr Harris asked. 'Just so you know what's making the noise.' He held his heavy, pyjamaed son with difficulty on his forearm and bent his head down to look into his face.

Huw said nothing, pressing himself against his father. A pall of smoke had descended, obliterating everything above the level of the garden fences, and from the vantage point of the patio nothing could be seen except the occasional white flash like the blink of sheet lightning. The noise, however, was continual, and clear as gunfire. It occurred to Dr Harris that soldiers in trenches in the First World War must have experienced something similar.

Huw flinched at every bang.

'It's a shame,' Dr Harris said at last, becoming irritated and already feeling guilty. 'I wanted to show you the rockets. Rockets are very beautiful. Very gentle, very colourful. I wanted to show you that there's nothing to be frightened of with rockets. You remember the gunpowder I was telling you about? When you see something and you know how it works you don't need to be afraid of it.' He looked up and round. 'It's a pity we can't see them with this smoke.' But as he spoke a rocket screeched down out of nowhere, shooting sparks onto the tiles, and exploding with a tremendous bang directly above the patio. Huw screamed and plunged, and Dr Harris staggered sideways, then backwards, and then forwards into the house.

He sat in his study again, with his computer off, looking at the screen. 'I am no father,' he thought. 'No more children for me,' he thought. 'One is enough, one is too many. I shall go mad.' He thought of Huw so tenderly his stomach seemed to contract. 'This is a farce,' he thought. Every morning, as he left the house for work, he looked up and saw Huw in Ffion's arms at the bedroom window, waving; and he would wave back, and in that wave was all he wanted or needed of love. But he was often exhausted. His temper was short. At the age of thirty he had discovered that he lacked common sense.

Was it parenthood that had made him so volatile and unpredictable, so fearful and aggressive and weak? The street was full of children. Every day he came home to find other people's children in his house. He worked all evening with children screaming round him. He got up in the middle of the night to tend to screaming children. He was woken in the early morning by children climbing into his bed and screaming for breakfast. Although he had only one child, it felt like many. He should be strong for Huw but he was weak.

Parenthood was a vocation of failure. He did not believe it.

'A vocation of failure,' he said out loud. 'I don't believe it.'

He sat staring at his blank computer screen. He would think despairingly like this, attempting to recover his hope and determination, his belief in natural order, until Ffion called him, when he would go back downstairs, into the chaos of domestic life.

Parkside is the southernmost suburb of the city, its houses occupying the middle ground of desirability between the smaller terraces in the east and the large villas in the north. The Harris's house was positioned midway in the longish road that gave the suburb its name, with the grander houses at the park end, and the humbler ones towards the main arterial road. There was some rented accommodation, and one or two student houses, but there was seldom trouble. Architecturally, the houses in Parkside Road were typical of late Victorian speculation, brick terraces of a standard design embellished with stained-glass doors and tiled paths and tablets of stuccoed swag above bay windows. Many were now encrusted with extensions, to the loft or into the back garden. Because there were no garages the road was permanently narrowed by parked cars down either side. There was some crime, mainly car theft, but not much. It was usually very quiet.

Dr Harris sat on the sofa in their back extension with a book and a glass of wine, arguing with his wife. Every few minutes fireworks whined and exploded outside. From upstairs he heard his son's misery. The back room, with its strip lighting, whitewashed walls, faded rugs and varnished floorboards, seemed violated, and Dr Harris said so. His work had gone badly; he had indigestion. Though he tried to remain calm he soon became irritable. In the kitchen Tom howled and hurled himself against the door with rhythmic thuds, and, in the few gaps between these noises, Dr Harris expressed the view that there was an undercurrent of violence running the whole length of Parkside Road.

'Everyone in this house,' he said, 'would benefit from a gram of temazepam.'

An air-bomb-repeater, or something similar, produced a shattering series of bangs outside the French windows.

Ffion poured him another glass of wine. 'This isn't

violence,' she said. 'I'll tell you what violence is. Do you remember the man at number twenty-five, the one with brown hair, married to the red-headed girl? Apparently two months ago he followed her to Greece and shot her, actually killed her. That's violence.'

Dr Harris considered this with an expression of contempt. 'I don't know who you mean,' he said dismissively.

'Brown hair, shy. Small head, long neck.'

'He wasn't married.'

'To the red-headed girl.'

'I wouldn't call it red.'

'Janine told me.'

'Janine?'

'Who comes to clean. What's wrong with you?'

'Alright!' he said loudly. 'I believe it! It's the silliest rumour I ever heard and I believe it. Anything can happen in this bloody street.'

'It happened in Greece.'

'You know what I mean.' He fumed, half to himself. 'This isn't a neighbourhood, it isn't a community.' He sipped his wine staccato-fashion. 'It's an echo-chamber.'

'It's not a good reason for hating the neighbours.'

Dr Harris felt an outburst coming on. 'The neighbours?' he asked sarcastically. 'They aren't *neighbours*, they're figments of the imagination. We're all figments of our neighbours' imaginations. That's what it's come to. We're anything they want us to be – murderers, red-heads, philanderers, dog-stranglers, whatever suits them. That's the reality!' He began to wipe spilt wine off the coffee table with aggressive, smeary gestures.

'What do you mean, "they"?' Ffion asked.

'Think about the implications,' he went on in a loud voice, ignoring her. 'Oh yes, what about the implications, let's be quite clear. If there's no real community, there's no collective sense of right and wrong, no social consideration, no idea of the common good. It's moral anarchy, it's the law of jungle. *That's* what we've come to. Don't pretend you don't know.'

Ffion sighed and got up.

'I'm being practical,' he said indignantly, as if she had denied it. 'You're always telling me I'm not practical. We know absolutely nothing about people who live twenty yards away, who we see every day. That's how it is. Other people? You can't get through to them, they're out of reach, they're in Greece murdering their wives.'

Ffion turned and walked through to the kitchen.

'For God's sake, I'm not saying I approve!' he shouted after her. He drank his wine and scowled. 'Who bought this wine by the way? This is awful wine. Why are you going? All I'm saying is, the wine is below average.'

Ffion was climbing the stairs.

'Of course they're in Greece murdering their wives,' he shouted after her. 'Where else do you expect them to be?'

*   *   *

At eleven o'clock, restless in bed, he wondered out loud how long it would be before the fireworks finished, how long the purgatory of the day would be extended.

'There's a party in the street,' Ffion said. She did not look up from her book. The glow from the bedside light turned her brown hair ginger. 'I can hear music.'

Dr Harris sat up. 'A party?'

'Probably the students,' Ffion said. She read her book.

'Jesus Christ.' He rolled his eyes.

'Don't wake Huw.'

'You can really hear music?' Dr Harris checked his watch.

'For God's sake,' Ffion said. 'Why are you always so angry?'

'I like being angry,' Dr Harris said.

Ffion sighed. 'It's so sad,' she said.

'I'll tell you what's sad,' Dr Harris said angrily. 'Of the few things left to me, anger is the closest to dignity.'

After a while they switched off the light, but Dr Harris lay with his head slightly off the pillow so that he could hear the noises from outside better. The music grew perceptibly louder. Twice he got out of bed, went over to the window and, with his face squashed to the pane, tried to see along the street. It was nearly midnight, and he was exhausted.

'All I want is some ordinary peace,' he said.

'You could go and ask them to turn it down,' Ffion said sleepily.

Back in bed, still irritable, he touched Ffion's shoulder with his arm as he rolled over, and the warmth slowed and soothed him.

The bed smelled of washing powder.

After a moment he put his face against his wife's back and curled up his legs so they fitted hers, and gave a sigh. 'Ah,' he said, and they lay quietly.

'I'm sorry,' he murmured, after a minute or two, in a very quiet voice.

'*Nos da*,' Ffion said, but he was already asleep.

At half past twelve there was a knock on the door, and he woke with a terrible taste in his mouth.

'Christ Almighty,' he said. 'What now?'

'Someone at the door,' Ffion said without opening her eyes.

There was another knock; then, almost immediately, another. He tried to find his dressing gown and slippers, couldn't, and went down dressed in two jumpers, mudstained track suit bottoms and his smartest shoes. The knocking was repeated several times until he opened the door.

A neighbour stood in the doorway, a fat man with a well-trimmed beard and large tinted glasses. After a moment Dr Harris recognised him, he had often made complaints about where Dr Harris parked his car. He did not know the man's name.

'I'm sorry to be the bearer of bad news,' the man said with obvious insincerity, 'but your car has been vandalised.' His glasses magnified his gaze which seemed accusing, and his voice was high-pitched. He

27

stood fastidiously on the doormat, his navy lambswool sweater pulled down over his broad hips.

Dr Harris, who took no care of his car at all, was annoyed that this man had disturbed him with such news.

'The police will be here in a minute,' he went on. 'But I thought you should know at once.' He made a gesture with his hands which Dr Harris did not understand, it seemed to signify either indifference or satisfaction.

'Where is it?' Dr Harris asked, having forgotten where he had parked it, looking past his neighbour up and down the street. He was very tired.

'They didn't move it,' the man said. 'They may have tried to, of course. They ran over it.'

'Ran over it?' Dr Harris imagined steamrollers. 'Christ Almighty. *Ran over it?*' The man was silent for a moment, though he kept his eyes fixed on Dr Harris who had a vague recollection that he was a churchgoer. 'Ran over it?' he repeated quietly.

'There are footprints,' the man said. 'On the bonnet, the roof and the boot.' He blinked. 'We're making sure they don't come back to wipe them off. I expect the police will get them with the footprints.' He turned away as if in disappointment. 'Obviously it is delinquents.' Just the sight of the man's back made Dr Harris furious. Then he noticed the other men, a small lynch mob of neighbours, waiting under a street lamp. Reluctantly he fetched his car keys, and went out.

One said, 'They did yours and that new chap's,

Ainsley somebody. We've knocked on his door and he knows but he doesn't seem to want to come out.' The man was drunk. Dr Harris did not know his name either, but he recognised him, having gone to his house twice in the last month to ask him to turn down his television. Drink made him deaf apparently.

'We don't need him,' the man said, looking at Dr Harris as if they didn't need him either.

Dr Harris raised his eyebrows.

'We'll get them anyway,' the man said.

'Who will we get?' Dr Harris asked. Already he hated these men.

The man nodded towards the end of the street, and Dr Harris became aware of the music again. 'Students,' the man said as if he might spit. 'They won't know what's hit them when the police get here. We'll show them,' he added, tugging on his trouser belt.

Dr Harris looked away and muttered under his breath. For a moment he stood glancing up and down, then he went along the street until he came to his car, and saw the roof was stoved in: a large dint the shape of an upturned oyster shell shone in the lamplight. The car next to it was the same. He felt only exhaustion. The drunk man who had unexpectedly come up behind him said, 'Slamming the door gets it out. Pops it up.'

Wearily Dr Harris unlocked the door, and when he slammed it the sunken roof popped up immediately.

'Usually works,' the drunk man said.

Police sirens wavered in the distance and faded.

'Now I'm going back to bed,' Dr Harris said.

'Oh no,' the drunk man said. 'The police will need details.' He put his hand on Dr Harris's shoulder. 'Don't worry,' he said soothingly. 'We'll get them. Don't you worry. When the police come we'll get them.'

Down the street the line of dim bay windows and gables and rooftops receded in a ragged V into the black-mauve sky, and overhead the moon was obscured by a few clouds the colour of silverfish. Despite the muted music from the end of the road, it was peaceful. The air felt damp and heavy. The five men waiting for the police to arrive stood in a shadow cast by a skip, muttering, their mood conspiratorial, and everything they said offended Dr Harris's sense of social consideration and common good. But he was tired and he promised himself he would say nothing. His plan was to achieve a weary indifference.

Though he recognised his neighbours he knew none of their names, and hardly anything about them. They were the fat man, the drunk man, the old man with a saintly expression and the tall man with white hair and no chin. The fat man seemed to bear him a grudge.

Sirens sounded again, but fainter still, as if going in the other direction, and the men stood in a group, talking and occasionally coughing.

'I'm sorry to say there are times when it seems we have to take things into our own hands,' the fat man said. In the lamplight his face was perfectly placid.

They all looked along the wet street towards the cheaper houses where the music was coming from.

The drunk man said, 'Not them,' and laughed to himself.

There was a pause and then the tall man with white hair and no chin said in an educated voice, 'I have a gun actually.'

They looked at him.

'I wouldn't like to be in the position, frankly, but I would shoot,' he went on mildly. 'Faced by an intruder I mean.'

There was a silence while they took this in.

'That's it,' the drunk man said disbelievingly.

'Lee-Enfield, circa 1895, magazine-loading, manufactured in Birmingham. Something of a rarity, though not uncommon in the auction houses. Been in the family for nearly a century. It still works, I check it occasionally. I'm not a violent man,' he added, 'but one needs to know one's rights.' It was not clear if he was being humorous.

Dr Harris bowed his head and curled his bare toes in his expensive shoes and concentrated on saying nothing. When he looked up the fat man was staring at him accusingly, and he stared back.

'I don't suppose you read in the *Telegraph*,' the man said, 'about the Frenchman who wired his car with explosives and blew them up when they tried to steal it.'

'Semtex,' the drunk man said promptly as if he had been asked a question. 'Plastics, whatever.'

'It's the sort of thing that wouldn't be allowed

here,' the fat man said, still looking at Dr Harris, 'and I suppose some would say quite right.'

'Golf club,' the drunk man said. 'I've got a golf club under my bed.'

They were all looking at Dr Harris. They seemed to be waiting for him to lose his temper.

'With a car like mine,' he said mildly, though with some effort, 'I don't consider murder an appropriate response.'

'You'd be surprised what kind of cars they go for,' the fat man said.

'You miss my point.'

'They ran over your car. They didn't run over mine.'

'That's not the issue.'

'I distinctly heard them go over it,' the fat man went on, as if Dr Harris had denied it. 'They made quite a noise. But it is right outside my house. I hope you don't mind me saying,' the fat man continued, addressing the group. 'It is a mistake to park your car where you can't hear it being vandalised.'

Dr Harris opened his mouth but there was a sound in the sky and they all looked up.

'Bloody hell,' the drunk man said with delight, and at that moment two police cars arrived suddenly at the end of the street with their lights going, followed by a Black Maria and a police motorcycle. The helicopter passed noisily overhead once and lifted away.

'Do they think it's a riot?' Dr Harris asked sarcastically, and the fat man looked back at him as he went down the street to meet them.

✱   ✱   ✱

After a while a policeman came over to Dr Harris, and they went together to his car and stood looking at it.

'The roof was in,' he explained. 'But I slammed the door and it popped up. It usually does,' he added.

As the policeman shone his torch on the car, Dr Harris looked at his watch and thought of his son. It was one o'clock, Huw was asleep in bed, his face looking blindly along the pillow or buried under the duvet. His stomach contracted as he thought of this. He pictured him as he would see him in a few hours, in Ffion's arms at the bedroom window, waving as he went off to work. His expression would be as conventionally solemn as a baby Jesus. It was an image Dr Harris used to calm himself when all else failed. There was a dank breeze off the river, and his feet were cold in his expensive shoes.

'No harm done,' he said automatically to the policeman, still thinking of Huw. 'I think I'll be getting back to bed.' Along the street the little group of men were standing next to the police cars, lit up with blue, and the sight of them made him angry. His son, he thought, was growing up in a neighbourhood of vigilantes.

The policeman continued to examine the roof of his car.

'No other damage sir?' he asked.

'No.'

'Any marks, scratches, footprints?'

'Footprints,' Dr Harris said without looking. 'As you see.'

'Sir?'

As Dr Harris stepped forward impatiently he noticed that the footprints had been wiped away. He remembered having done this when he popped the roof back up.

'Only a few,' he said. 'And rather blurred. Is it important?'

The policeman looked at him and Dr Harris wearily shrugged.

First the policeman inspected the bonnet, then the boot. Ignoring Dr Harris, he called over another policeman and for a while they talked in low voices.

Dr Harris looked at his watch furiously, and imagined telling his neighbours what he thought of them. 'Have you found anything?' he asked the policemen.

The first policeman gestured with his torch again and he went forward to the front of the car.

'What is it?' he said.

The policeman gestured again.

On the bonnet there were some scraps of something, purplish and crinkly. He raised his eyebrows.

'Kebab,' the policeman said.

Dr Harris bent his head towards him. 'I'm sorry,' he said. 'I don't think I heard.'

The other policeman was writing out a form. 'Kebab,' he said as he wrote. 'A scattering.'

'Kebab?' Dr Harris said. '*Kebab?*' The policemen were busy, and Dr Harris raised his eyes to the sky. 'Yes, it would be, of course. Why not kebab? There has to be something we can get angry about, something we can pin on someone, there's no reason it shouldn't be kebab.' As one of the policemen looked up, he fell silent, and began to chew his bottom lip. He stared down the street to where his neighbours stood.

While the policemen went to the house where the party was, perhaps to issue warnings, perhaps to haul out suspects, the five men waited on the pavement. Four of them were talking of crime. The fat man described the alarms he had fitted to his car and his house.

'They can cut off an alarm,' the saintly-looking man said, 'like that. An alarm is nothing to them.'

As he listened, Dr Harris attempted to recover a sense of detachment; he imagined himself saying, 'You shouldn't worry so much. Try to remain calm. It's only fear that's making you talk like this.' But he thought of the policeman holding up the piece of kebab.

The fat man was talking about the litter that was thrown into his garden which the drunk man thought was an insult. Nothing, not even encouragement, perturbed the fat man in his steady condemnation of students, delinquents and – it seemed to Dr Harris – people like him who did not take care of his car, who parked it in front of other people's houses. The cold breeze carried smells of wood smoke and gunpowder, though all the bonfires had gone out and the fireworks lay wet and charred in gardens and the park.

Dr Harris, trying to ignore the fat man, imagined himself saying, 'Listen, I can understand your concern,

I can even sympathise. It may be a question of right and wrong, but not of vindictiveness and prejudice. We live in a neighbourhood, not a corral.'

'I'm very sorry, but it must be stopped,' the fat man said. The pitch of his voice seemed actually, physiologically, intolerable.

'By the way,' he said, turning to Dr Harris. 'Did they notice that your tax disc is out of date?'

'My tax disc isn't out of date,' Dr Harris said indignantly.

'I'm sorry but it is. You're lucky if they didn't notice. It is, after all, an offence.'

There was a silence in which Dr Harris imagined saying something wise like 'How can we hope to bring our children up to be thoughtful, tolerant and clear-sighted if we fear what we don't understand, if we hide behind prejudice, if we judge others harshly without a thought of our own transgressions, if we make the scattering of kebab a punishable offence?' And then he said, 'Fuck you.' He had not meant to say it, but it sounded good to him.

There was a pause. 'Now, now,' the man with a saintly expression said.

'Fuck you too,' Dr Harris said. 'And you,' he said to the tall man with no chin. 'My tax disc,' he said to the fat man, 'is fucking well not out of date.'

The fat man hit him. This wasn't what he had expected at all. Stepping forward quickly the man threw a wide, girlish punch and hit Dr Harris on the ear. There was confusion. Dr Harris roared as he wrestled with the fat man in the road. Hands grabbed him from behind and he struck out, shouting. Once he felt the fat man's beard against his face, and he roared again. Then, quite quickly, it was over, and he was suddenly still. Two policemen were holding him against the side of a car while he panted and grunted. The fat man, held against another car, was screaming, 'I want to press charges! I want to press charges!' And, more appalling and ludicrous still, he could hear himself shouting back, 'You fat fucker, I'm going to rip your fucking beard off!'

One of the policemen clapped his hand over Dr Harris's mouth, and forced him through a car door, and he wriggled round and pressed his face against the pane, still shouting. Then suddenly he was quiet. Every window in the street was lighted. The fat man had stopped shouting too, and there was a sudden deep hush. Dr Harris sat on the cold back seat of the police car with his face against the glass, bewildered and heaving, trying to work out what had happened. Up at his bedroom window Ffion was standing with Huw in her arms. He could see, in the light of a street lamp, his son's pale impassive face looking down at him; and, as the car started to move away, before he could stop himself, he was waving to him, waving his hand at his son from behind the window of the police car. But his son wasn't waving back.

# THE DREAMER

After his wife left him David Worral began to have strange dreams.

It was 1992, early September, the last of summer. The season would not be affected by his wife's desertion, but he was losing track of time, it slipped away from him. He worked for the county council in the cashiers department, and each morning he put on his bicycle clips and safety helmet and cycled slowly to work. His everyday life was banal in the extreme though his dream life had become intense. He went past the redbrick Victorian church, past the arts and crafts vicarage with its Tudor arches and steep front gables, past the park where he used to walk with his son, past the lawns, the lake, the tennis courts, the putting green. There were fourteen different types of tree in the park, some of them exotic. As usual, the weather was confused, hot flushes of sunlight clashing on the grass with dark shadows of clouds. Along the edge of the lake the willows were still green, the water smooth and shiny. Mallards sunned themselves on metal pipes which ran out from the bank, and at the far side, where the railway bridge rose like old machinery from a break in the overhanging hawthorn, two grebes swam shyly with a late brood of chicks.

He dreamed he was in an old house with draughty corridors, clanking lavatories and windswept lawns. The interior walls of the house were stippled with textured paint and when he brushed his arm against them, he bled. All the rooms smelt, whatever the season, of unwashed carpet, not an unpleasant smell but as persistent and indefinable as an air of sadness. The kitchen was too grand, the living room too cramped, and the shabby, colonial furniture (*chaise longue*, drinks cabinet, magazine rack) had an air of dust-sheets about them. There were mirrors everywhere, tarnished and filthy: on the landing, in the dining room, on the stairs, on the kitchen door, in the entrance hall – and he was never sure exactly how many people were with him. There were some strangers and a man he understood to be his father. Except for his father they all seemed to be children. The period was immediately post-war, a time completely unknown to him; the plot consisted of badly-lit scenes of intrigue, midnight assignations, whispered conversations and inexplicable moonlit diggings in the lawn. A moaning wind accompanied everything. In his dream David Worral slept alone in an attic room decorated as a nursery and littered with the relics of someone else's childhood: a scuffed rocking horse, a battered tin spinning-top, a Pinocchio with one foot. The dream ended when his father held up a soft toy and announced, 'This rabbit is soaked with semen.' He had never been to the house, he had never had an attic nursery, he had never owned a disabled Pinocchio or wet toy rabbit – it was as if the dream belonged to someone else.

Towards the end of September the warm summery weather abruptly ended and a week of winds blew most of the leaves off the willows, carpeting the water yellow at the edge of the lake. The swallows had gone, the Canada geese had not yet arrived, the swans with their gross cygnets lorded it over the mallards and coots. David Worral's wife had taken Philip, his three-year-old son, to her parents in Brighton. He could no longer remember when this had happened, presumably it was recent but already it seemed part of an irrevocable past. Although Mary Worral was prepared to speak to him on the telephone she would not permit him to visit. Whenever she talked on the phone, she would ask him darkly what he was going to *do* about things. The cat was behaving oddly, it had defecated twice in the cupboard under the stairs.

Neither his wife's desertion nor the memories of his son would impede the spoilation of autumn. He clung to his routines similarly. He put on his bicycle clips and helmet, and cycled – though now sometimes unsteadily – past the park on his way to work. Cypresses and Scots pines along the edge of the path were black against the bright sky like inky calligraphy, as insistent and unintelligible as the memories he suffered as he went.

There was a wide, ragged lawn between flower beds and shrubberies where he had often played football with his son. Not actual football. David Worral would toss the ball to him and Philip swung his leg and sometimes connected with the ball. His eye was good, sometimes he kicked the ball over David Worral's head, or into a flower bed or shrubbery. One day he kicked it into a silver fir.

'Where has it gone?' Philip asked.

David Worral hunted round the tree, squinting up. Sunlight flashed off his spectacles. His forehead shone.

'You find it,' Philip said.

Philip was a solemn boy with a slow, impassive face. He stood behind his father like a copy of him, his head upturned, a hand on his hip, frowning the same frown. 'You get it,' he said.

David Worral took off his glasses and wondered about climbing the tree. It was very spiky. He was not a tree-climber by nature, he was a neat and careful man whose dress sense was conservative, who had been called by his wife a blighter of impulse and instinct. He was without imagination, she had said. The thought of struggling blindly in the prickly interior of the fir tree distressed him. He saw himself as his son might see him, eyes squeezed shut, face averted, legs kicking feebly like an insect.

'You climb up, Daddy,' Philip said.

David Worral shook the tree instead, saw the ball bounce suddenly free, and something fell into his left eye. There was a strong smell of resin. His eye began to water.

For several minutes, in the patch of shadow under the fir tree, he crouched on the ground in great pain, massaging his eye, Philip standing next to him in an elderly manner with his arm on his shoulder.

'Can't get the bloody thing out,' David Worral said in a restrained voice.

'Bloody thing out,' Philip repeated solemnly.

'Sorry,' David Worral said after a moment. He took his hand away and his face was wet. Philip bent and put his face round to see.

'Don't be sad, Daddy,' he said. He withdrew, and added thoughtfully, as he looked away towards the lake, 'You love me very much. That makes you happy.' His voice was high-pitched, but measured.

October came, and with it rain. The leaves that remained on the deciduous trees turned gold and ruby and lemon-yellow; the dripping park crackled with the colours of a wildfire. There were high winds, at night. By now David Worral made no secret of his drinking.

When he drank he was perfectly in control, he did not remember; he stared at the television, receptive to the formal qualities of the pictures and unconcerned with their meaning. Sometimes neighbours surprised him by knocking on his door late at night to ask him to turn the television down. One was the humourless doctor. One was a man with a precise beard and eyes enlarged by bifocals, he did not know his name, he had forgotten it; his name had gone with David Worral's wife and belonged to a different time. To himself he called him Mr Nosey. Before, when he was living with his wife and son, it would have embarrassed him to be spoken to like this, but now he experienced such moments, like the television pictures, at a remove. He no longer called out 'Good morning' or 'Nice weather,' to his neighbours but waited for them to come to criticise him. His dreams had taught him that images are random and free of context.

He dreamed that he had just murdered Maradona, the famous footballer. There had been a disagreement in a pub, he had picked Maradona up by the ankles, a small, stiff figure resembling a trophy, and broken him in pieces on the floor. Then he was outside in a crowded street, naked. His nakedness seemed part of a plan he had forgotten. It was raining hard. He turned off the street into a yard, and as he crossed it a blue-and-white child's ball bounced in front of him and he caught it in his hand and carried it with him. Suddenly at the end of the yard was a vast slope of mud falling away in the distance to forest, and above it, like a mirror, a black sky. Rushing forward, he skidded onto his knees and churned downhill, gathering speed until he woke.

After a few weeks he telephoned his mother-in-law and his wife answered.

'I want to see you,' he said. 'I want to see Philip.'

'I told you. You can't.'

He could hear her breathing into the receiver and, in the background, Philip shouting.

'I have to talk to you, Mary,' he said, trying to make out what his son was saying. 'There are things we have to discuss.'

'There are things,' she said, 'you have to *do*.'

He was listening hard to his son.

43

'Hurry up,' she said. 'I have to give Philip his bath.'

He thought he heard his son asking who it was on the phone.

'What is he saying?' he said.

There was a scraping sound as his wife put the phone against her chest and he heard her shout, 'What, again? Are your socks wet too? Take them all off. Take everything to the linen basket. Take it now.' Then the line came clear and she said to him, 'Well? I've things to do.'

Realising she was about to put the phone down, he said without thinking, 'I have these dreams.'

There was a pause, and she said, 'I don't want to hear about your sexual repressions.'

'I can't stop dreaming, I've never had dreams like them.'

'You sleep,' she said. 'Count yourself lucky.'

'They make no sense. They're not about you. Last night I dreamed I was attacked by a hooded figure in the street.'

Mary Worral was silent.

'The street was steep and cobbled and rainwater was running over the cobbles, it was a street I've never been to. I struggled with the figure and I pulled off the hood and it was Kruschev. I know nothing about history, I don't even know what Kruschev looks like, I just know it was Kruschev. These are the dreams I have. They don't mean anything, I just have them. I don't want to have them anymore.'

His heard the hiss of his wife's breath. 'Do you

44

want to say anything else before I hang up?' she said.

'No,' he said.

Then she hung up.

Midway through October there were violent storms, heavy downpours out of bright skies, water falling from the blocked eaves of the vicarage in sparkling curtains. Half the sky would be clotted with black clouds, half a razzle of sunlight. Shadows lay across the bright grass like spilt ink. Floodwater lay in dazzling pools on the lawns. Sometimes the air smelled earthy, sometimes metallic. The willows and whitebeams were stripped of their leaves, exposing the scribble of branches; the cypresses and Scots pines were broad, black strokes overshadowing the path. What were they trying to tell him, he wondered. He wanted them to tell him something, give him something to believe in. Without belief he did not think he could do the things his wife wanted, he didn't think he could carry on. But he believed in nothing. Gulls, foraging inland, criss-crossed the lake, their shadows sliding on the cloud-stained water, and the humpbacked coots toiled through the tiny waves. David Worral noticed all these things with a clarity he had not known before, weaving to work on his bicycle, without bicycle clips or helmet, his expression entranced. In the years he had lived in Parkside he had never loved it, but now he adored it, finding beauty in everything. Twice, while cycling through the park, he collided with other cyclists; once he fell off in front of a neighbour who helped him up and pleaded with him to see a doctor. She was pregnant and had a toddler by the hand, and a blind terrier on a lead, and looked so exhausted he felt that she, not he, should see a doctor. She was married to the doctor in fact, which made David Worral angry and confused, and he cycled off without thanking her.

There were scratches along his forearms where the cat had attacked him.

The whitebeams in the park lined the tennis courts on the lake side. Once, he remembered, when he and his son had been picking blackberries they had been caught in a summer shower and had taken shelter under the end tree. He remembered how they sat on the earth with their knees under their chins, holding each other tightly, hunching their shoulders and craning their heads forward as if they were peering out at the barrage of rain from the end of a tunnel. A mist of water jumped on the paths and the fourteen types of trees smoked and the pitted lake looked like a patch of milk-coloured gravel. Overhead, the rain drummed in the leaves. In David Worral's memory it was an exhilarating moment, like the dissolution of everything earthly; he had half-expected to be granted an insight, of what he had no idea.

As the rain eased, Philip saw a squirrel clinging to the side of the tree next to them, its damp fur dark and tufted.

'A squirrel there,' Philip said. It twitched its tail and disappeared. 'But where has it gone to?' Philip asked.

They both looked and David Worral stood up.

'Into the leaves,' he said. 'It's sheltering from the rain.' The rain was stopping.

'I want you to show me that squirrel.'

They peered into the trees, moving slowly along the row. His son kept telling him to show him the squirrel. Eventually the rain stopped altogether.

'I think it's gone home,' David Worral said at last, and, turning, saw the squirrel balancing on a bramble bush near where they had been sitting. 'There!' he shouted, much more loudly than he intended, and the squirrel leapt, twisted and fell into the bush, and Philip burst into tears. Remembering this, the squirrel seemed to prefigure some calamity in its twisting fall, and the sound of his own voice was pure dissonance, like a flaw in the memory itself.

Every night he dreamed, ludicrous dreams he was embarrassed to remember. He remembered them in sharp detail. Analysis was irrelevant, as if the dreams were simple aspects of a terrible world more real than this one. Every morning he woke in horror to Parkside, and said to himself, 'That's not it, that's not what I'm looking for at all.'

In late October it was dark when he cycled back from work along wet paths shining with puddles of reflected yellow light from the street lamps, streaks of shifting moonlit silver across the lake to the massed blackness of the hawthorn at the far side. At the county council offices the chief cashier took him aside and asked him if he thought he should take a break. His manner was valedictory, elegiac and vague. It seemed that there were problems concerning the hours David Worral was keeping. Complaints, of an unspecified nature, were alluded to. 'Really David,' the chief cashier said, 'you have to *do* something. There are people you can see,' he added. Looking away, he murmured, 'People who know about addiction, who can help.'

So October came to an end with tranquil skies and cool breezes, rooftops and trees sharp against pale light; frail violet cyclamen mixing with rusty leaves in the flower beds in the park; robins, wrens and blue tits exploding out of the long beech hedge that concealed the untidy vicarage garden. Blue days and white sunlight. David Worral stayed at home, existing in the limbo of an indefinite leave of absence. Often he sat at the window, looking out onto the street, but he had forgotten who everyone was, his neighbours were strangers and he could not understand them. Why were they continually going into each others' houses? Who were the old people who came to their door to collect packages? Who were the youths who rode around on bicycles peering into parked cars? Had he once know them?

Whenever his wife answered his call he would hang up, but he rang every day until one afternoon his son picked up the phone.

'It's Daddy,' David Worral said. 'Don't tell Mummy.'

There was quiet, he could hear his son breathing.

'It's Daddy,' he said again. 'Can you hear me? Is she there?'

'Mummy told me not to talk to you,' his son said and was quiet.

'I'm your Daddy, Philip,' David Worral said. 'You can talk to me. You can whisper.'

'But I don't want to whisper.'

'Alright, you don't have to whisper. Are you alright? I love you. I love you so much. What are you doing, what did you have for lunch? What's the matter now, is she there?'

'Why are you whispering?'

'Listen. I miss you. Do you miss me?'

The boy was quiet.

'I miss you,' David Worral said, realising at that moment he had nothing further to say, terrified that his wife would take the phone before he had a chance to think of something. His urge to talk was so intense that tears came to his eyes. Without thinking he said, 'I have these terrible dreams.'

'What dreams?' his son asked promptly.

'These dreams.'

'What dreams, I want you to tell me what dreams.'

'I dream I'm alone in a big house.'

'What house?'

'A big house with lots of rooms and fancy lawns and everything is old and wet.'

'What rooms? What is wet?'

There was a sharp noise, and his wife's voice said in a hiss, 'I'll call the police. If you call Philip again, I'll call the police. You're sick, you're trying to frighten him with your sickness. When are you going to do something about *yourself*?' She hung up. Staring into the receiver, he thought not of his wife nor of his son but of his dream, of the big house, of the wet lawns, of the toy rabbit soaked in semen. These things were real, and the others somehow were not.

In November the weather was bright and cold for a week, and then the gales began. They were worse even than the October storms, they blew down exotic trees in the park and ripped the fencing away from the tennis courts. Tiles came off the badly maintained vicarage roof. The empty lake heaved. All the birds had gone. David Worral walked round the park, stepping over the wreckage of branches and fencing, head down, butting into the slanting rain, this world, like the other one, lying in fragments around him. He was not often sober.

Once, when he was, he telephoned his parents, an elderly couple shocked by his separation but clinging fiercely, as if there were nothing else left, to sympathy.

'How are you?' his mother said.

'A bit tired.'

'You can talk to us about it,' his mother said. 'Whatever it is, you can tell us, we're your parents.'

'It's the nights,' he said.

'Don't drink if you can help it,' she said. 'It's the worst thing. Have you tried sleeping tablets?'

'I sleep. But I have these dreams.'

'It's inevitable. This dreadful separation, it's bound to come out in your dreams.'

'The dreams have nothing to do with it. Not that I

can work out. I don't understand them at all. Last night I dreamed I went on a coach trip. We were driving into the mountains. The scenery was spectacular, ranges of blue-coloured peaks like the ones you see in postcards, with forests and lakes and waterfalls. All of us on the coach had packed lunches, and as we drove we ate them: sandwiches, hard-boiled eggs, crisps, bars of chocolate. In a way we were children, but we weren't childlike. Then the driver turned on the radio and there was an announcement that nuclear war had broken out, we had three minutes to get to a shelter. The bus pulled up in front of a mountain lodge. It was made completely of glass and inside was an enormous circular swimming pool. There was no water in it. Without being told what to do, we all knelt round the pool, bending forward with our heads down and our arms dangling in as if we were learning to dive. This was the official position. We were all naked. It was very peaceful, almost religious. I noticed that the woman next to me had a beautiful back; there was something about her back, a vulnerability. Then we heard vague distant noises, dull booming sounds, and I sat up. This is the strange bit now. In the distance, one by one, the blue mountain peaks were turning red and exploding. Like fireworks. As I watched, nearer peaks began to glow, then nearer ones, then the nearest. Finally we were going to die. A shower of huge boulders was dropping onto us, I saw the boulders very clearly, they were dropping in slow motion onto the glass lodge, and at the last second I knelt down again with my head hanging in the pool and heard them crash through the glass roof and felt them strike me in the back, but very softly, like a sprinkling of warm ashes. And then I woke up.'

There was a long pause. He had the impression that his mother was making hand signals to his father; he could imagine the expression on her face.

'Oh Davey,' she said at last. 'What *are* you going to do? What about taking a holiday somewhere?'

In the terminal month of December – the month he would always, afterwards, remember – freezing fogs rose from the lake and spilled into the park. Christmas approached, the season of sacrifice and renewal. Shrubberies and flower beds vanished in the fog, trees stood in puddles of mist as if levitating. Bird calls rose eerily out of nothing like the voices of spirits, laughter and hooting from far away, the metallic chink of coots like hammers on tin, the creaky-door noises of honking geese, and when they stopped the only sound was the dripping in the leaves. Sometimes, standing at the edge of the lake, David Worral saw the swans. Their blotched cygnets seemed caught in the throes of an ugly transformation, something both slow and abrupt, like the transformations in dreams. He spent hours sitting on a bench staring into the mist, remembering the times he had come to the park with Philip. Whenever he thought of his son he could not stop himself smiling, a twisting grin which made him appear demented. Sometimes he moaned out loud. Joyfully he remembered walking with Philip by the lake, the water changed in different weather, creamy under rain, cracked and dazzling in the sun, flat and polished reflecting clouds and gulls, raspberry red in the sunset. It made him cry to remember the smallest details: flaky red paint on the sides of the paddle boats on the pond, the peculiar skip of the three-legged dog which never seemed to have an owner. Nostalgic and sentimental, he remembered the people he and Philip used to encounter: the old men with their model boats, the park keeper with the sunburned face in his floppy hat and sandals, 'the boys' from number thirty-four sunbathing discreetly on matching towels laid out on the grass beyond the putting course, the elderly woman with elegant hair who used to swim at the lido, despite her age. (The woman's name was Mrs Hurrell; he was surprised to remember it, it was two years since he had seen her. At the age of sixty she had married a penniless young Turk, and had gone to live abroad. She was elegant and articulate and old; it upset David Worral to think of her marrying for sex.) Suddenly, on the park bench, he was seized with the fear of dying, dying for no reason, for nothing, dying without a murmur, with dreamlike indifference.

Christmas was coming on, the season of parties. In the street he saw dishevelled costumed children returning home with bags of sweets and toys. A boy with ginger hair the same age as Philip stood on the pavement staring up at a silver balloon in the shape of a dolphin which he held on a string, watching its slight bright movement against the drizzle. Thoughts of Christmas afflicted him, of goodwill, of family;

memories of Philip on Christmas morning kneeling in his pyjamas in front of a pillow case full of toys, struggling with wrapping paper, struggling with boxes, looking round for help.

All the minor faults in the house that should have been repaired in the summer were exposed by the bad weather. The rotten window frames let in water. The blocked drain in the back yard overflowed and stank. The east-facing panels of fencing in the back garden which had been teetering for some time finally collapsed onto the flowerbeds, and dead leaves piled up on them.

The cat had left him. He sometimes saw it in the street but it ignored him. He did not think he could bear to live and witness these ruptures, he did not think he could survive Christmas. But at least – he reasoned – he could be out of the country.

He went to a travel agent and read their magazines. Lanzarote was a small island off the coast of North Africa made entirely of volcanoes with beaches of black sand and no natural water. There was not a tree on the whole island, an amazing surreal place. It was not Christmas there. He booked a last-minute package holiday in a self-catering apartment, and three days later was sitting by a swimming pool drinking beer and reading out-of-date English magazines. All his neighbours were hanging up Christmas decorations and swapping recipes for turkey and duck. It was eighty degrees Fahrenheit. For long periods he put his head back and stared up into the sky. He had aged five years.

The sky over Lanzarote was always empty, the colour of bed sheets. Warm breezes blew across tawny-coloured land, raising dust from building sites and roadsides and hazing the distance. Whatever he had expected to be there was not, but there was a Laundromat, a café and a bar, a volleyball court, a beach (golden, not black) and a partially covered sewer. Such details were fragments no different from a Scots pine puddled in fog or a boy kicking a football: they would never form a new whole. For that, he looked to his dreams. His dreams horrified him, but only in them was he fully himself. By the swimming pool he wore a white hat with a floppy brim which he had bought at the airport shop, and every morning he smeared insect repellent on his neck, shoulders and legs. He was on holiday after all. In the evenings he sat in the bar talking to the barman who was Irish and an English barber who had bought a time-share in the apartment next to David Worral's.

'My wife wouldn't fly, I'd given up all chance of going abroad,' the barber said. He was a fat, bearded man whose khaki shorts and white shirt were immense. 'I came home one day and she said, "I've cancelled the Cornwall holiday, we're going to Lanzarote." I had to look it up on the map, I'd no idea where it was. It was a bit of a shock seeing it just off the coast of Africa with the Sahara desert right next to it, and when we got here my wife said, "Oh God, what have I brought you to?" It was a hundred and twelve degrees. I hadn't been abroad before and I didn't know what was what. When I breathed in it wasn't like breathing. It was like, I don't know. Stifling, you could say it was like stifling.'

Every year the barber dressed up as Santa Claus. He had a daughter, a vulgar, raving beauty with no apparent interests. She wore black bikini bottoms and cutaway T-shirts in pink or yellow or blue. Her finger nails were badly bitten. On the third night David Worral asked her to go to a beachside club with him. There was a Christmas Eve party.

They arrived very late, harassed and self-willed, like strangers thrown together by mutual disappointment. The Beach Palace was very noisy, though there was no obvious source of the noise — it seemed generated, like everything else, by the heat. The darkness was spasmodically lit by disco-lights. People with burned faces whose eye orbits had been kept white by sunglasses stared out of the shadowy recesses. The woven straw roof shivered above the jumping clientele.

After a few drinks David Worral and the barber's daughter went with their cocktails and walked on the beach.

He was unshaven and his face was puffy. Earlier in the afternoon he had fallen against a cupboard in his kitchenette and cut his forehead. Overhead, the stars were massed so tightly they seemed to obscure the sky, as insistent as the disco and the karaoke. Waves hissed at their feet as they walked, moonlight on the bay making a snail's trail out to sea. David Worral staggered. When he finished his cocktail he stretched back his arm and threw the glass in a high arc into the sea, and heard a half-hearted cry in the background – 'Hey!' – but the barber's daughter just shrugged. Nothing he had said or done all evening had raised a flicker of interest in her. She had stared the other way while he talked at length about his separation, his children, his wife. Those fragments. There was a pain in what he imagined was his liver which he minutely described as if trying to prompt her diagnosis. Her beautiful lip curled when she bent her head to sip her cocktail through a straw. Trivial details such as these awoke in him a violent passion. When she could be persuaded to talk she talked, like her father, about their time-share, but with bitterness, complaining about the financial aspects, the inconveniences, the broken promises of the landlords, the boorish holiday neighbours like himself, the lack of amenities, the inadequate maintenance agreement. Her tone was enraged and vindictive. She was wearing tight white trousers, and a lemon elasticated tube which squashed her breasts across her chest, and nothing else; she was the sexiest and most difficult woman on the island.

Twice, walking along the beach, David Worral tried to kiss her. Once he fell over. Eventually they came to a row of sunbeds and rested, the barber's daughter silent and sullen, David Worral silent and exhausted. He surrendered himself to his exhaustion and lay back, his resistance gone, and closed his eyes, trying to empty his mind of the meaningless fragments of his immediate surroundings. When he sat up again the barber's daughter was looking at him with pure scorn, and it came back to him who he was. He thought that in a second she would get up and leave him there, and he did not care.

'In a little while,' he said in a voice almost sober and quiet, as if to himself, 'I'm doing to do something about all this. But at the moment I can't, I have these dreams which stop me. Last night I dreamed that I was in a group of men walking through the streets of a foreign city. I didn't know any of them, but we were all part of a football team. Our behaviour wasn't good. After a long time we came to a house, and in this house was the girl I was in love with. The girl wasn't there, but her mother was. Her mother was awful. There was a long wait for the girl to come. I made egg sandwiches for tea. Still she didn't come. We all sat round the table with her mother drinking tea and talking – but I'd left the sandwiches outside on a plate in the road. I could see them, but I was too embarrassed to say anything. While I was watching, a van slowly reversed over them, and I got up and said quietly, it was almost as if I were talking to myself, 'Excuse me, I must just rescue the sandwiches.' The girl I was in love with still hadn't come but I knew what she looked like, she was a thin, dark-haired girl wearing a navy blue pencil skirt and a thin pullover in the same colour, and she had a habit of running her hand through her hair and keeping her face hidden, as if she was afraid of being recognised.'

He fell silent. Expecting her to get up now and walk away, perhaps to run, not looking back, he was surprised to see her turn to him with a look of fierce complicity.

'Egg sandwiches?' she said. She clutched his wrist. 'That's nothing. I have dreams all the time. Last night I dreamed of angels. Not bloody egg sandwiches! *Angels*!'

'Oh God,' David Worral said. His eyes were bright and blurred. He looked at her with horror, putting a hand on her arm, or perhaps her leg, listening to her talk aggressively about the angels in her dream.

That night he dreamed he was digging a flower bed in his garden in Parkside Road. Sunlight shifted at his feet through the filter of leaves of a chestnut tree, and from other gardens he heard the squeals and splashing of children in paddling pools, and a radio playing classical music. Near him Philip sat on the grass, thoughtfully but ineffectually attacking the lawn with a plastic spade, sucking in his bottom lip and frowning. As David Worral paused to look at him, his wife came through the French windows onto the patio carrying a jug of lemonade. 'Refreshment for the workers,' she said. Her smile was like a flash of sunlight itself. He was about to say something, but at that moment the bells of the church began to ring, a placid and musical rhythm, and with a feeling of terror he woke up. He was in his hot room in the apartment on Lanzarote. The sky was the colour of bed sheets. There was a warm breeze blowing across the tawny-coloured land, raising dust from building sites and roadsides, and hazing the distance. It was Christmas morning, and for the first time since his wife left him he began to cry.

# A SHORT HISTORY
# OF ROMANTICISM

## I

At five o'clock in the evening on a wet Thursday in January, Jeremy was in the front room of his house in Parkside Road throwing things into a bag, in a hurry to finish before his wife came home. He had been married six months. His wife was a beautiful, sensitive, red-headed, intelligent woman, and he hated her. The curtains were undrawn, anyone passing might have looked in and seen him in the bright cage of the room, as cutely self-absorbed as a hamster on a wheel.

Outside it was freezing and damp. Oily snow lay in the gutters from the heavy falls at the end of '91.

Realising, even as he struggled with the bag, that this was a seminal moment in his life, Jeremy took a last look round. The room inspired fresh hatred. He hated the melted-chocolate-and-honey-swirls carpet, he hated the cheap door with the plexiglass handle that would not close, he hated the freckles of damp above the skirting board by the doorway. Now that he thought about it, he realised that he hated everything about the house with its useless, ugly improvements and pre-war wiring. He hated all the other smug-faced houses in Parkside Road too; in fact he hated the whole neighbourhood with its cosy park, two post offices and three pubs with royalist names.

But most of all he hated his wife. They had had an argument. He fingered the bruise on his forehead where she had hit him.

In the bag were a pair of running shoes, some sportswear, the three-piece suit he had worn at his wedding, an oven-ready meal in its aluminium tray, a handful of cassettes and an economy tub of E45 cream. Since childhood his skin had been dry.

Every few minutes he looked at his watch. It was a quarter past five. His wife would not be back till seven thirty, but Jeremy always allowed himself a two-hour margin for everything he did. Thus the logistics of leaving his wife, and the time it was taking, panicked him in a way that the decision to leave had not. In his imagination he already saw himself sleeping under one of the exotic trees in the park, weirdly lit by moonlight, abandoned and abandoning like all lovers. It was no problem, it was even satisfactory. But the process of leaving was fraught. Rapidly scanning the bookshelves, he chose for his exile the least readable book he possessed, *A Short History of Romanticism*, and threw it into his bag.

When he had moved into Parkside Road three months earlier he thought he was leaving one life behind and beginning another. Twenty-eight years old and newly married, he walked with his wife down the road looking in at all the bay windows. The houses were modest but their renovated interiors were stylish and desirable. The knocked-through front rooms had stripped floorboards, spotlit prints on the walls and restored stucco detail on the ceilings. Jeremy and his wife had counted fourteen pianos, seven original fireplaces, five *chaise longues*, two antique writing bureaux, eight rocking chairs, three footstools and one life-size porcelain bust of Beethoven. Women in ski-pants sat curled on sofas with their feet under their haunches, men in canvas recliners watched portable televisions on wall brackets and toddlers built wooden brick houses on Peruvian rugs in front of real fires. There was even an authentic gay couple. These were the elements of a peace no less deep for being banal. Jeremy and his wife watched the mothers going along the street with babies and children, the fathers drawing up in their mid-range Volvos and Volkswagen Golfs, late from the office, carrying in packages from the wine shop. In the evenings the babies fed and slept, the children played the piano with perfect postures, the parents opened a bottle of Pinot Noir and sat in their extensions planning the restructuring of the garden. Jeremy's neighbour on one side was an elderly man with a saintly expression and a spiteful sense of humour, and on the other a placid middle-aged woman with elegant hair who spent all her time in the garden. Jeremy and his wife thought they would feel at home in Parkside.

Now he knew that it was not possible to have a life

there. His wife still had to find this out. He glanced at his watch, picked up his bag ready to leave, and stopped abruptly.

A glass lamp had fallen off the loudspeaker by the window and smashed. The wreckage of dusty shards lay like a patch of weeds on the carpet. He stared at it. Who had done this? Could it conceivably have been him? He knew exactly what his wife would think, his wife would think that, like burglars who smear their excrement on the walls, he had smashed the lamp in the urge to dirty what he was leaving her with. In fact he felt precisely this urge, so he went guiltily into the kitchen, fetched a brush and pan, and began to clean up.

Jeremy, unfortunately, was a compulsively tidy person, and when he finished with the smashed lamp he noticed how messy the room was. Before he knew what he was doing he was hoovering the carpet, stacking magazines and newspapers, emptying the wastepaper baskets and wiping the surfaces with a damp cloth. By the time the room was clean it was six o'clock, and he was behind schedule.

At the front door, on the point of leaving one life behind and beginning another, he allowed himself the luxury of imagining his wife arriving in an hour or so and finding him gone. He saw the hallway as she would see it (desolate, bereft); the front room (empty, tidy) where she would perhaps stop and call his name; the kitchen (quiet, deserted) where she would sit and eat her lonely meal.

Her lonely meal? Turning with a frown, he went

quickly back down the hallway and opened the fridge door. The fridge was empty. For a full minute he stared at it, then at his watch, then at the fridge again. Who had taken all the food? His wife, no doubt, would think that he had deliberately left her with nothing to eat, a last mocking gesture. As she knew, mocking gestures appealed to him. Moaning, he dropped his bag and ran guiltily for the car.

When he returned from the supermarket it was seven o'clock. Leaving his wife was proving to be as difficult as living with her. The dinner-time hush lay over Parkside, and mauve clouds were sinking slowly down the dark sky towards the roofs of the last houses in the street, as slow-moving in their escape as Jeremy in his. Cursing his wife, he loaded the fridge with food: an onion tart in a plastic tray, a bag of mixed salad, three sardines in dill sauce from the delicatessen counter, a lime sorbet, a plastic pot of zabaglione, some cheddar and a few, slightly bruised plums. He slammed the fridge door and shuddered. His wife would rejoice to see him dead, she would smile to see his bloated corpse dredged from the lake into which he had flung himself, his trouser pockets stuffed with metal, rocks, gravel – but *he* had left *her* with food.

'I am a martyr,' he said, 'to my principles.' He did not consider what these principles might be. It was ten minutes past seven and he was panicky. His wife was on her way home but at last he was ready to leave.

At the front door once more, looking back on his life with a clear conscience, he again imagined his wife arriving home in about (he looked at his watch) a quarter of an hour. This time he saw her stopping in the doorway and sensing his absence, dropping her satchel, and running in panic down the hall into the kitchen to find his note. It was a pleasing thought. But he paused, staring. There was no note. What had happened to his note, how could he have forgotten to write a note? Jesus Christ! Not even a note? Glancing at his watch, and moaning again, he ran back down the hallway to the kitchen.

For five minutes he turned the room upside down looking for pen and paper, and then, for a further five, he stood twitching at the table without a thought in his head.

Something from Saul Bellow was on the tip of his tongue, but he couldn't bring it to mind.

Eventually he scribbled, 'Ever fallen in love with someone, ever fallen in love with someone, ever fallen in love with someone you shouldn't've fallen in love with,' added the postscript, 'The fridge is stocked,' and ran in panic out of the house.

As he rushed down the path, his neighbour, the elderly virtuous-looking man, was coming the other way. He nodded to Jeremy's bag. 'Leaving home?' he said, and laughed.

Many people saw Jeremy in his flight from Parkside, they came to their windows to see what the noise was. It took him five minutes to manoeuvre the car out of the space into which it had been blocked

since he returned from the supermarket. Parkside
– his last view of Parkside – appeared to him in
fragments in his rear-view mirror, terrifying glimpses
of claustrophobic walls and hedges, gable-heavy roofs
and wedged cars, all toppling onto him, preventing
his escape.

Only when he had swung out onto the main road
did he let out a sigh. The sight of long stretches of
unsullied snow on the water meadows at the side of
the road raised his spirits.

'Free at last,' he said out loud, and at that moment
he glanced towards the pavement and saw his wife
looking at him. He let out a scream. He had no
chance to crouch, or cower, or compose himself.
There was an extended moment in which he felt
his face run through every expression of frustration,
anger, cowardice and disbelief; then he was swerving
to avoid a van, driving through a red Pelican Crossing
and accelerating in second gear out towards the ring
road and the thickening sky.

## II

The Lodge at the Hill was chilly. Jeremy let himself
in and stood in the whitewashed hallway, bag in hand,
uncertain what to do.

'Hello darling, I'm home,' he said and listened to
the quiet.

There was a smell of laundry, but it was only
the damp, no one had lived there since he had left

a year earlier. Still carrying his bag, he went up the stairs and looked round, opening all the doors cautiously as if he might find someone asleep in a bed. Everything was as he remembered it, except that downstairs the dining room had been renovated and the sideboard repaired. The chandelier had been removed. Otherwise, with its colonial furniture and tarnished mirrors, the house gave off the same air of shabby gentility and bad luck.

'Perfect,' he said out loud and the silence closed round his voice.

The owners, Emeritus Professor Sir Ernest Booth and his wife, who lived in the big house, had decided not to let it again after Jeremy had left, preferring to keep it for guests. Jeremy had been allowed to keep his key. Why the Emeritus Professor and his wife should like him so much he could not understand, but they had told him again and again that he would always be welcome to stay there. At the moment, they would be in Spain where they wintered every year, and there was no need for him to explain his position until they returned at the beginning of April.

After some time he found himself standing in the middle of the living room still holding his bag. First he took out all his things and arranged them neatly along the wall between the bookcase and the fireplace; then he put his ready meal in the oven, opened the front door and sat on the step, smoking cigarettes in the cold, damp air. It was dark but he could see that the garden, still largely covered in snow, had grown wild:

visible patches of lawn were rank with clover; dead clematis hung crisply from the chestnut pole arch; the bird bath of weathered granite was listing badly and would soon collapse into the bed of roses. The only sound was the plip–plip–plip of drips. There was something pleasant in all this. Jeremy told himself that he was refreshed by the violence of nature, delighted by the savagery of its growth and decay. Violence, like love, was seasonal, erupting and subsiding in its time. He smoked four cigarettes, one after the other, occasionally fingering the bruise on his forehead, then went inside and discovered that he had forgotten to switch on the oven.

When he returned from the off-licence he was shocked by the complete darkness of the Lodge which was hidden from the road by a barricade of beech trees. Darkness alarmed him, he could never sleep alone without waking in the middle of the night to listen for the slight, familiar sounds to turn into footsteps and whispers. Thinking of the night ahead, he stumbled twice as he went across the short stretch of grass to the door.

'Not yet,' he said grimly. 'Soon.'

He put the bottle of whisky on the coffee table and got a smudgy glass from the renovated Edwardian sideboard.

'Here's to me,' he said. He had a couple of drinks, and said, 'Free at last.'

An hour later he had finished a third of the bottle

and felt completely sober. The taste of the whisky nauseated him, and the freezing chill of the house made him shiver.

Slowly, another hour passed. The television did not work.

Eventually he was forced to admit that he was not enjoying himself.

He was by his own admission an unreconstructed romantic. He understood and appreciated the elation of abandonment and exile – but he could not concentrate on these things, the damp spoiled it for him, settling onto him like an icy dust-sheet as he fidgeted in his armchair. For forty minutes he struggled with *A Short History of Romanticism*, and reached page six. It mainly comprised protracted quotations in a variety of languages unknown to him. He lost his way in Tasso, Goethe, Schlegel's *Lucinde*, the *Psychologische Fragmente* of Novalis, Chateaubriand's *Atala*, Janin, Holderlin, and the more or less impenetrable antics of the English flagellant Swinburne. It was not recent scholarship. It was all interesting, but revolting.

The damp eventually drove him from the chair, and he hovered in the doorway, swinging his arms to keep himself warm, not knowing what to do. Looking at his watch he saw that it was only nine thirty, though it seemed much later, and he tried to imagine what Sarah would be doing. Would she have phoned the police? Would she be walking the streets looking for him? Would they be dredging the lake? Parkside was not very far from the Hill, in fact it was right below it, probably the lights of the Parkside houses could be seen from one of the bedroom windows. Jeremy was halfway upstairs before he angrily stopped himself and went back down to the living room. Sarah would not be walking the streets, she would be telephoning – telephoning her mother, her brothers, her best friends, her colleagues, her once-a-week badminton partners, her acquaintances at her Modernism in European Literature night classes. By morning his desertion would be as well known as if it had been announced in the local newspaper. He almost grinned. Perhaps the whisky had affected him more than he realised. With sudden lightness of heart he began to change into his sportswear.

'My only regret,' he said as he jogged up and down, 'is that note.' Breathing deeply, he stretched, twisted, grunted. He wouldn't feel the cold so much after a jog.

Country lanes are dark and most lack pavements. Melting snow made the conditions treacherous. He set out with confidence. The wet night air was freezing in his nostrils and lungs, invigorating in the same shocking way as a cold shower. For a while he ran with a long, loping stride along the road which bordered a golf course, then took a track past a farm and down a hill. Fields fell away northward towards the city, wet and black like mud, and the black overhanging sky was filled with vague movement. He often slipped on patches of ice, and twice fell. Quite quickly a pain developed in his left side. A storm was coming on. Panting badly, he entered a wood and the track narrowed until he was pushing his way through brambles. It was very dark, but he was in the mood to continue, despite his pain and the obvious futility, and he stumbled on recklessly, changing direction each time the path divided, catching his feet on rocks and logs and ducking clumsily under branches. A manic determination to force himself into the tightest, blackest corner of the wood seized him, and he pushed forward, on and on, until the path finally petered out altogether and he was forced to a halt, bent double in the dark, up to his knees in briars. 'This is it!' he thought. 'This is the real thing!' The pain in his left side racked him and his head ached. He was soaked from the wet undergrowth. For several minutes he crouched there heaving, exhausted and apathetic. Thunder broke in the distance and he wondered if he could make it back before the rain started. Sharp smells of moss and earth made him cough, aggravating his pain. He remembered he was drunk, and began to shiver.

'At least I'm not lost,' he said, into the darkness.

Rousing himself, he cautiously went forwards twenty yards, stopped, turned ninety degrees, went on for ten yards, turned about and retraced his steps until with difficulty he came back to his starting point. He paused, listening. All round him in the wood were tiny sounds, but he could see nothing beyond the immediate patch of undergrowth, and he had no idea where he was. 'What about Novalis?' he asked himself. 'What about Chateaubriand, Janin, Holderlin and Swinburne? Did they get into scrapes like this?'

From time to time thunder broke again, and whenever it died down he heard something else, like an echo of the thunder that never faded. After a while he realised that it was traffic on the ring road, and he began to move slowly towards it. He could not stop thinking about Sarah. Was she blaming herself? Had she opened the fridge door and wept to see the lime sorbet and sardines? There would be moments over the coming years when she would start out of her chair with the thought of them. He imagined her sitting on that chair, naked under her dressing gown split above her crossed knees and he could not stop himself thinking of her sexually; the image of her richly built indifferent body almost made him cry, and he went more quickly through the undergrowth, not caring that his legs were slashed by brambles and his face whipped by branches, as if pain would relieve him of his thoughts. 'She kills me,' he thought. 'She really kills me.' Vaguely he wondered what she would think if she could see him now.

By the time he reached the ring road, his legs were lacerated and his face bruised. The pain in his side was worse and he was nauseous. As he emerged from the wood and climbed over a low timber fence to the road, it began to rain heavily.

It was the threatened storm. Sheets of rain swirled onto the tarmac like force fields of electricity and cars rounding a steep corner from the north burst through them with a bang and receded, trailing spray, up the long, slow curve south. Jeremy shivered at the side of the road, soaked and hunched, still thinking of Sarah.

He was trying to work out why he had married her; he had hardly known her. In any case, as soon as they married, she had changed. In six months she had changed completely. He had not thought it possible to change so much. Several minutes went by and the traffic was dense. Rain ran down his neck, his shorts, his socks.

He remembered that at college his best friend had once attempted suicide on a busy road. Shutting his eyes, counting to fifty, he had run suddenly into the traffic. Jeremy imagined it: the sudden screaming of brakes, the shouting, his friend tripping up the far curb and falling onto the pavement. He had suffered a sprained ankle. The girl who had prompted this remained indifferent to him – after all, he hadn't been killed. A cautionary tale. Jeremy thought of his wife. She wouldn't be phoning the police or searching the streets for him, she wouldn't even be telephoning her family and friends with the news. She would be curled up on the sofa watching television. Her dressing gown would be open to the thigh and she would be humming to herself.

Closing his eyes, Jeremy began to count.

He counted very slowly. In between numbers he drifted into fantastic thoughts. 'She will love me,' he thought, 'but it will be too late.'

Every few seconds he heard a car go past, there was never a moment when the road was clear. He counted the last ten numbers as if everything depended on it, every muscle in his body tense, and when he reached fifty, without moving, he opened his eyes and saw that the cars were all in the distance to the south, sounding nearer than they were, and the road was totally clear. He set off across it, and when he was halfway a VW Golf came suddenly round the corner, churning out spray and giving him a fright.

It took him an hour to walk back along the hard shoulder of the ring road up to the Hill. It would have been quicker to walk into Parkside. It rained all the way, and when he arrived back at the Lodge he was soaked and shivering.

'Hello darling, it's me,' he said. His teeth were chattering and his voice was adenoidal. The house seemed quieter than ever. In the harsh white hallway he saw himself in a mirror, his hair plastered down his forehead, his legs blotchy and criss-crossed with cuts, his face pouched and mottled. He held his arms away from his sides and walked stiffly towards the mirror as if he had wet himself.

'Just as long as you can keep your sense of humour,' he said in his mother's voice, and he went upstairs to run a bath.

### III

Some time later he remembered he had not switched on the hot water and went back downstairs.

It was late, eleven thirty, and he felt he had been in the House of Calamity for days. It was even colder than before. Wrapped in a duvet which he had discovered in the airing cupboard, he sat in the dark thinking of his wife. The duvet smelled of curry. The whisky bottle was two-thirds empty and he was still sober. Though he tried, he could no longer remember what the argument with his wife had been about, he only remembered his rage and sense of persecution, both of which had dissipated.

'I'm reduced to this,' he thought, but there was no comfort even in pathos.

Sleep was impossible. Wondering if his wife would be able to sleep, he pictured her sleeping soundly, lying on her side, her red hair like a red veil over her face. Perhaps, he thought, he should telephone her to let her know he was okay. He would prefer to torment her.

Shivering, he got up out of the armchair with the duvet round him, and went into the dining room where the telephone was. It was working. He toyed with it for a while, then dialled and waited.

'Hello?' Sarah said. 'Is that you?'

'Mrs Wilson?' he said, holding his nose.

There was a pause. 'Yes,' she said.

'Is your husband Jeremy Wilson?'

'Who is this please?'

'This is PC Philip Fenny at Thames Valley Police Headquarters. I'm sorry to disturb you, Mrs Wilson, at this time of night. I won't keep you long. But we have a slight problem you might be able to help us with.'

'Is it about Jeremy?'

'We have a man here at the station, Mrs Wilson, and we need an identification.'

'Oh God, what's happened? Has something happened to him?'

'There's no need for alarm, Mrs Wilson. As I say, what we need is an identification so that we can get Mr Wilson home. We can do it over the phone. It's purely formal procedure.'

She interrupted him. 'Is he alright then?'

Jeremy paused, thinking. 'The problem is, Mrs Wilson, one of our officers brought him in this evening, and at present he seems rather confused.'

He could hear her breathing, he imagined her mouth slightly open, her hair falling over her face, her expression clouding; he imagined her pressing the receiver to her ear. He tried to imagine what she would be thinking.

'What's he done?' she said. 'Has the silly idiot hurt anyone?'

He ground his teeth. 'No, no, Mrs Wilson, it's nothing like that I assure you. He's resting at the moment. If I can just ask you a few questions so we can get the identification out of the way.'

She interrupted again. 'He wasn't here when I got home, I didn't know where he'd gone. Where was he when you found him?'

He thought again. 'Do you know the Tesco's superstore out on the ring road? he asked.

'Yes,' she said.

'He was on the roof.'

'On the roof? Oh God, the *idiot*. What do you mean "confused"? Please let me talk to him.'

'I'm afraid that's not possible at the moment, Mrs Wilson, he's with the doctor.'

'The *doctor*? Oh God! What's he done to himself?'

'Mrs Wilson, if I can just get an identification from you we'll see if we can get him to the phone. All we need is a brief description. As I say, it's just formal procedure. Take your time.'

There was a silence, as if she were gesturing to someone in the room, though he knew there could be no one there.

'Mrs Wilson?'

'Jesus,' she said. After a moment, she said, 'He's about six foot, he has brown hair.' She faltered. 'Brown to fair. I mean fairish.'

'Yes. Colour of eyes?'

'Brown. Or green. I'm not sure.' She fell silent. 'I'm sorry,' she said after a moment. 'I've never done anything like this before. I'm a bit emotional.' She paused again, apparently to collect her thoughts. 'When he went to work this morning he was wearing grey corduroy trousers and . . .'

'I wouldn't worry about what he was wearing, Mrs Wilson, when we picked him up he was naked.'

'Naked! Jesus Christ!'

'Let me ask you this, Mrs Wilson. Does your husband have any unusual features?'

'Yes, he's an idiot.'

Jeremy bit his lower lip. 'I mean physical features, Mrs Wilson. Any unusual physical features?'

'No. Unusual? No, of course not.' Now she was becoming impatient.

'Nothing at all?'

'He's just ordinary. He's about as bloody ordinary as you can get. Not that he thinks so.'

There were signs of strain in her voice.

'A final question, Mrs Wilson. Has Mr Wilson suffered any injuries recently?'

She hesitated. 'No,' she said.

'No blows to the head?'

She was silent.

'The reason I mention it is there's bruising on Mr Wilson's head, Mrs Wilson. He can't account for it himself. It's nothing serious, but the doctor thinks it may have caused his confusion.'

He could hear Sarah holding the phone against her chest, and muttering, as if she were talking to someone.

'Hello, Mrs Wilson?'

She was crying now, making a sound like frying in a pan. 'What is the bastard doing to me now?' she wailed. 'Tell that bastard . . .' And then she broke down.

'Mrs Wilson,' he said, 'can you hear me? This line's very bad. Hello, Mrs Wilson, are you there? Hello?' And he cut the connection.

Some time later he found himself in the darkened living room with the empty whisky bottle in his hand, he didn't how long he had been there. He wanted to cry, he stood there trying, but he couldn't. Instead he threw the bottle suddenly through the glass front of the Edwardian sideboard, and glass flew into the room with a bang. He began to throw other things after it, his book, his running shoes, even the economy size tub of E45 cream. There wasn't much to throw and he soon stopped.

Then he was standing holding a large shard of glass over his wrist. He still couldn't cry. Disgusted, he threw the glass into the wreckage of the sideboard and sat down, very tired. Wrapped in the duvet, with the stink of vindaloo in his nostrils he almost fell asleep on the carpet, but it was too cold.

At one thirty he got up and began to retrieve his belongings. He put everything, including the remains of the whisky bottle, into his bag. Upstairs and downstairs he methodically wiped a cloth over all the surfaces he might have touched and put the duvet back in the airing cupboard. He was exhausted, he could hardly move. His hands were numb with cold. On his way out, he fetched a screwdriver from a box under the kitchen sink and smashed the front door lock, and left the door ajar.

It was still raining heavily. For a while he sat in his car shivering, smoking cigarettes while the wind rocked the car to and fro, and raindrops shattered on the dark windscreen. He told himself that he believed in forgiveness. Then he slowly drove home through the rain, not knowing that when he got there he would find nobody in.

# METAMORPHOSES

## I

It was February 1996, and it had been raining all month, dreary rain out of dull skies. Anyone driving north into the city towards Parkside went along a causeway between flooded fields, the blown water marked out with stubs of fence posts, and here and there flecked white with riding gulls. In the city the drains were blocked, and winds drove more rain out of the dirty sky against streaming roofs and streaked windows. Gutters overflowed and the pavements were brown with puddles.

Carefully avoiding the puddles, Mr Polunin went across the small courtyard into the museum, lengthening his stride and swaying as the hour chimes rang out, a tall, thin man wearing a mackintosh and a slouch hat. His hair was prematurely white and he had no chin. His manner was refined, exaggerated by the bad weather.

The women of the Ladies' Arts Society were waiting for him at the entrance to the Western Art Collection, a fussy, attentive crowd. His expression did not alter as he took control, and when he spoke to them he leaned back, head averted, as if he were addressing not the Ladies' Art Society but the portrait of John Tradescant the Younger, founder of the collection, which hung on the wall of the antechamber behind them. To the Ladies, Mr Polunin, with his fastidious disregard, was as good as a historical character himself. He finished speaking and, without inviting comments, turned and led them into the gallery, swaying again, one hand on the lapel of his blazer like a public figure in a Victorian illustrated newspaper, the studied tilt of his head giving him an air of otherworldliness. He went without a glance past the pictures for which the museum is famous – Utili's *Flight of the Vestal Virgins*, Uccello's *Hunt in the Forest*, Giorgione's *Tallard Madonna* and Bronzino's *Portrait of Giovanni de' Medici* – and stopped at the *Salmacis and Hermaphroditus* by Piero Vagnetti called Giocattolo, a stark pre-coital scene on cracked panel. He began to speak almost before the Arts Society Ladies were ready with their notebooks and pens, again looking past them, seeming to fix his gaze on the fifteenth-century *Martyrdom of Saint Peter* ascribed to Luca Della Robbia hanging twenty yards away on the far wall of the gallery, an object – at that distance – accessible only to the imagination. Evasion was his habit, as all the Ladies knew: he looked neither at the people to whom he talked nor at the pictures he talked about. Scarcely ruffling the hush of the museum with his well-bred, watery voice, and picturesquely posed between a Florentine *pietra dura* cabinet from the mid-seventeenth century and the Giocattolo, he seemed almost an exhibit himself.

There was a smell of damp clothing mingled with perfume, and a faint odour of polish.

'The Baroque,' he began, 'is, in many ways – very many ways – a consequence of the Reformation, although perhaps one wouldn't deduce this from the painting here. The subject, one instantly sees, is pagan.'

They wrote: *Baroque-Reformation*, and under that: *Pagan*.

'This is the *Salmacis and Hermaphroditus* by Giocattolo, an Italian painter of the late sixteenth century. A minor painter, but instructive, I think. Much of what he painted is lost; this picture is one of three identifiable, surviving works. One doesn't know much about Giocattolo's life, a few facts, nothing more. He was born in Milan, or somewhere near Milan, perhaps Pavia, between 1578 and 1581. In 1597 he was in Rome working on the Palazzo Farnese commission with Carracci. Around the turn of the century he was imprisoned pending an inquiry into the death of his mother – an unusual case, deaths of women not commonly subjects of interest at the time – and when he was released on probation he fled to Spain. Then in 1605, in Seville, he is reported dead. He was perhaps only twenty-four. One understands that this is the stuff of legend.'

They wrote next to the artist's name: *Died 24*.

'Circumstantial evidence points to the fact that the picture was painted prior to 1600. Very likely, *Salmacis and Hermaphroditus* is one of the many paintings produced in Rome in the latter half of the sixteenth century to satisfy the demand for scenes of mythological love. There were numerous collectors of pornography. The commissions would have been lucrative.'

He paused, but the women wrote nothing. Some of them allowed themselves to wonder which school Mr Polunin had been to, which social circles he moved in; there was something so English and *obsolete* about his manner. From the direction of the foyer there was the sound of raised voices, and a few of the Ladies turned their heads; but Mr Polunin went on lucidly.

'The title of the painting is taken from Ovid's *Metamorphoses*, one of the great literary works of Imperial Rome, as you know. As you recall, Hermaphroditus was the son of the deities whose names he bears, Hermes and Aphrodite: that is, of thieves on the one hand, and love on the other. I refer to sexual passion. Salmacis was a water-nymph, quite lowly. No doubt their story has the ring of archetype.'

Running footsteps sounded in a nearby gallery, then stopped. More of the women looked round or exchanged puzzled frowns with each other.

'In brief,' Mr Polunin continued regardless, 'Salmacis falls in love with Hermaphroditus, and when he resists her she forces herself on him, and in their struggle she calls out to the gods never to part her from him, and her wish is granted, to the degree that they physically merge – actually, physically, bond. They form a creature, if you follow, with both sexes, male and female. In other words a hermaphrodite.

Thus the twin themes which preoccupied Giocattolo in his brief career are announced: personal identity and sexual passion. And, of course, the interrelation between the two.'

They wrote: *Ovid*, or: *Hermaphrodite*, or: *Passion* (*sexual*) – and as they were scribbling two skinheads jogged into the gallery, one with tattoos on his face, the other wearing army fatigues, apparently looking for something to damage. Their appearance in the Edith B. Whitehorn Gallery of the Western Art Collection was for several seconds unbelievable. When the skinheads saw the Ladies of the Arts Society they stopped and stared at them, as if astonished. Astonished, the Ladies stared back. There was the shocked attention that is sometimes given to art. Then one of the skinheads made a farting noise, and panicky gestures of disapproval animated the Arts Society Ladies. This was not what they paid for, this was not one of their entitled privileges. The attendant, so officious when dealing with people who viewed the paintings too closely, had vanished. 'Excuse me,' one of the Ladies said, with a protective glance towards Mr Polunin. 'This is a private lecture.' The skinheads walked towards them.

'Now then,' Mr Polunin said, and the skinheads stopped, as if aware of him for the first time. The Ladies murmured appreciatively; there was a discernible expectation that he would take charge of the situation. He fulfilled their idea of dignified authority, an authority which derives from breeding. But he was not looking at the skinheads, he was still gazing towards the *Martyrdom of Saint Peter* at the far end of the gallery. He said, 'Let us consider the use Giocattolo makes of this rather hackneyed theme.'

Several Ladies tried to attract his attention, but they were aware that he did not encourage interruptions. 'What is interesting,' he went on, ignoring them, 'is the painting's dramatic effect. The clash of contrasts, the conflict of opposing principles. It may be said that such drama epitomises the Baroque.'

With goose-like cries of disapproval, the Ladies of the Arts Society skitted sideways as the skinheads pushed forward and went to stand in front of the painting. They stared at it, then, turning their heads, at Mr Polunin, so close to him that they could have butted him without moving. Bizarrely, he still appeared not to notice them.

'What might one make of the two figures?' Mr Polunin said without the slightest change in his tone of voice, and seeming almost, in his lack of focus, to be referring to the skinheads. 'The one so predatory, the other so demurely passive.'

Both skinheads turned sharply to the painting as if to read in it the meaning of the situation. There was a momentary intellectual impasse.

Mr Polunin gave a little cough, and went on, 'One naturally perceives, after the superficial shock of the coarse sensuality, that the clash is not between good and evil (a much overused formula in the time of the Baroque, as indeed in our own) but between the real and the ideal. This is the central drama. Note the pictorial contrasts which reinforce the point:

the turbidity of the lake though the weather is tranquil (this is, unmistakably a lake of evil); the presentations of the two figures, rear and frontal; the shaft of sunlight which irradiates Hermaphroditus, the shadows from which Salmacis emerges. Let us be clear: this is a painting at war with itself. Its subject is conflict. Our inquiry must be into the precise nature of this conflict.'

'This cunt,' one of the skinheads said, with a nod. 'This cunt cracks me up.'

There was a hiss from the Ladies of the Arts Society, and one of them walked away, heels clicking, saying, 'We simply cannot have this. I am going to fetch an attendant.' The rest remained, as if mesmerised by Mr Polunin's performance. They were not sure whether it was fear or sheer refinement that kept him talking about the painting of which they had all forgotten the title and subject.

'There is,' Mr Polunin continued, 'an intriguing compounding factor to the drama which is biographical. It is this. The features of Hermaphroditus are probably Giocattolo's own.'

'Talk about bollocks,' one skinhead said to the other, accidentally appearing to engage with Mr Polunin on the question of self-referentiality.

'In fact,' Mr Polunin continued unpeturbed, 'Giocattolo's use of autobiography in his pictures constitutes one of his main contributions to the development of the pictorial arts. In his other surviving paintings – two pietas – the features of the dead Christ are his own, and the Virgin Mary's are his mother's. Naturally,' (he waved a hand) 'one makes of such facts what one will.'

He paused, as if to allow the Ladies of the Arts Society to make the appropriate note, and the skinheads began to talk among themselves.

'What's this ponce on about?' one said.

'This bollocks about pictorial,' said the other. 'I've a fucking mind to do him.' They were grinning at each other, with childish malevolence, but at that moment the woman who had left for help returned with two attendants, saying, 'We are certainly not accustomed to such interruptions.' This, at last, was the real conflict. The skinheads turned, snarling, and Mr Polunin said suddenly, 'But consider the theme of sexual metamorphosis.' The attendants froze, and the two skinheads, as one, thrust their faces back at the picture. 'Here,' Mr Polunin went on smoothly, 'we have the painter's own face on a hermaphrodite body. A personal statement amounting to an affront to all recognised conventions of the day.'

In the uncertain pause that followed, the woman who had gone for the attendants, now confused, said unnecessarily, 'There they are.'

The skinheads turned. 'Fuck off,' one of them said. 'We're busy.'

'We're having a good time,' the other said. 'So fuck off. Come back later.'

They turned back to Mr Polunin.

'Go on,' they said.

Mr Polunin put his hand up to his mouth to contain a soft belch.

'Go on then,' they said.

There was quiet. Mr Polunin slowly shifted the angle of his head so that he could have looked, if he had chosen, at the skinheads. But he did not look at them, nor at the Ladies of the Arts Society, nor at the attendants hesitating nearby. They all looked at him. There was prolonged silence in the Edith B. Whitehorn Gallery, as if a prelude to some final confrontation, to a reply that Art – as it were – might give to Reality. Though his gaze was set into the middle distance and his expression was professional, a vein suddenly stood out in Mr Polunin's neck. Everybody seemed to be holding their breath.

'*In nova fert animus mutatas dicere formas corpora*,' he said.

The skinheads and the Ladies of the Arts Society looked at him in alarm.

'Filth,' a skinhead said. Mr Polunin said nothing. He seemed to have come to the end of his talk.

'Just filth,' the skinhead said again angrily. 'Just fucking munchies, tits and arse.' He seemed violently disappointed, on the verge of actual violence, but he had gone too far. Roused finally, not by this slur of Giocattolo, but of Mr Polunin, the Ladies of the Arts Society, encouraged though not led by the attendants, rounded on both skinheads and drove them back towards Uccello's famous *Hunt in the Forest*, an exhilarating moment of collective determination.

There was uproar.

Mr Polunin paused. He stood alone at the end of

the gallery, there was no one to see him totter. At the other end, the Ladies, the attendants and the skinheads were shouting. The whole scene was as distant to him as a picture, a tavern brawl by Bruegel or Van Leyden, dusty bodies, a lowering sky and a crow in flight.

He put a trembling hand up to his face as if to check whether any part of it were broken. There was in fact still so much to talk about, about the Spanish Baroque, the Counter Reformation, the rise of Realism, Velasquez and Zurbaran, but he turned unobtrusively to the exit, conveniently near, and went unsteadily out of the gallery.

## II

Because he had never learned to drive, Mr Polunin always took the bus when he went to see his mother. He sat upstairs, impeccable and abstracted, an incongruous spectacle among the schoolchildren, trying not to breathe their cigarette smoke, holding his briefcase on his knees, gazing out of patches in the fogged windows at blurred impressions of the street. He had a horror of so many other people so close to him, packing the seats round him, sweating, breathing and mingling. The journey to the nursing home took twenty minutes, and was part of the ordeal: his mother was eighty-five years old and not in her right mind.

They were replacing the drains again. Trucks and

diggers roared in their wire compounds; on the shattered pavement giant yellow plastic pipes, glossy with rain, waited in stacks against the time of their burial, and people carrying umbrellas and shopping bags went by without a glance. It was four o'clock in the afternoon, getting dark, and the traffic was slow. Headlights illuminated columns of rain. The road was lined with elegant Victorian villas, now seminaries and language schools, their rooms subdivided into offices, their gardens full of cars. Looking out on this, he thought of himself as if he were not fully part of the scene but a fragment to be examined in isolation, like the corner of a partially destroyed picture. The stink of damp clothes and cigarette smoke made him cough, a handkerchief held to his mouth. He considered with some anguish the decline of his career.

He was only forty-eight but he looked older, and he was old-fashioned. Connoisseurship was a discredited mode of art history. A younger historian would not talk of incalculable effects on later painters, of brushwork, of *tenebroso*, he would apply new theories, he would refer to semiotics, psychoanalysis, social history; he, more often than not she, would write articles entitled 'The Gendering of Public Space' or '(Dis)Membering the Female Nude'; from a statistical analysis of the Roman civic records for the year 1599 a whole system of artistic patronage would emerge.

He wondered about Giocattolo's mother, hypothesising motives for her murder.

The shops were busy all day. Rain ran down

their awnings, down hoardings, pillarboxes, telephone kiosks. In the distance black clouds against
the maroon sky seemed to be sinking onto it all,
like a loss of memory. Mr Polunin's family had had
pretensions, and, improbable though it seemed, he
was a rebel, the black sheep.

Giocattolo's mother's name was not known. No
marriage documents existed. Her age when she was
murdered could have been thirty or fifty, and she was
probably a prostitute. For some reason she followed
her son from Pavia to Rome, perhaps to support
him, perhaps to take advantage of his success. Did
Giocattolo want to escape her? Did he, the man
who sold mythologies of lust to Rome's degenerate
nobility, want to blot out the shame of her trade,
and was murder the only freedom he could imagine?
Could he perhaps have foreseen that flight, exile and
early death would be the consequence? Life had been
a brief but bitter series of conflicts for Giocattolo;
from the beginning he had surrounded himself with
lurid stage props – stormy nights, lakes of evil, jealous
deities, weeping mothers.

Mr Polunin thought in contrast of himself, of
his own props – picture galleries, bus rides, nursing
homes. He thought of Parkside Road where he lived
in a house built for Victorian clerks. He thought
of the people he had known, of Jean Hurrell, his
neighbour for twenty years for whom he had always
harboured a secret fondness. Another missed opportunity: he had always been too cautious to trust to
the larger emotions, preferring – still – to gratify the

smaller ones. For thirty years he had done nothing, his life had stagnated, he had never risked change. He coughed again into his handkerchief, thinking vaguely of the blaze of Giocattolo, the brief flare of other people, the drizzle of his own life.

Beyond the shops: flooded fields. Past the flooded fields: an office-block – rows of windows up a wall. Most of the children had got off the bus by now, leaving behind puddles of litter in the aisle. The bus went on to a former village, now a suburb with a new road running through it. There Mr Polunin alighted and stood thinking, breathing in the last burnt tang of diesel, before walking towards the nursing home.

At the reception he wrote his name in a book, and went down a long corridor into a glass-walled lounge furnished with high-backed chairs, a fish-tank and a television. His mother was sitting on her own in a corner, talking, her gaze ranging over the carpet. Two other old women sat in front of the television asleep. He walked past them to his mother, kissed her on the top of her bald head, and sat down.

'Queensland,' she was saying, 'has the most mar-vellous stamps, simply marvellous, mauves and greys and, I don't know, blues, marvellous. They were in perfect condition, if I had them now they'd be worth a fortune.' Her voice was wonderfully posh.

The television droned quietly.

'You're looking well, mother,' Mr Polunin said. There was a smell of sweat.

'I know what I wanted to tell you,' she went on

without looking at him, 'about the time we rode on the *khud* above Gulmarg, through the pine forests and flower meadows, do you remember, do you remember the smell of the resin and the androsace, and right above the forest I drank from a stream and, oh, the water, it was the most marvellous water, I've never tasted water like it since. And then those horsemen rode up, I remember now, they had the palest horses and the palest hair and brilliant blue eyes, they were huge, the horses were, oh, thirty hands high, and the men were giants, they looked down on me as if to say how did you get to be so small? Giants, like we used to be before we got so minuscule, I don't know why, I think we've starved ourselves if you want to know the truth, we ask for money before we feed anyone, but that's the wrong way, we should feed them first and then they would pay us.'

He leaned forward and adjusted her shawl. 'I don't want you to catch cold, mother,' he murmured. The room was warm. The smell choked him.

'Of course the grown-ups never associated with the natives, that was the word, associated, it's a word I've never had time for, why give them a name like natives, it never made sense to me.' She spread her imploring arms wide to the room.

He looked at his watch, glanced at the television and put his hand up to his white hair. His hand trembled. What he felt, suddenly, was the force of trespass, not the trespass into this place of dying, but into his mother's continuing life. The thought of her life – its quantity and solidity – frightened him. The thought of his own life frightened him too.

'Oh I remember,' she said, smiling, settling back, 'we went to Srinagar because we wanted to see the herons fly. Well, the road is very bad at that time of the year but we had a picnic, all of us had something to carry, and oh the dust, the dirt, that road was the worst road in the whole Raj, Daddy used to say, but when we got there there was a beautiful meadow and a river and the mountains of course, the blue mountains, they were so numerous and big, so very big, we hardly ever noticed them and when we did they seemed not there, I sometimes said I thought they were a different kind of thing altogether, a vision like the visions you have when you're tired, I don't know why, and Daddy laughed, and when we got to Srinagar, you'll never guess. There were no herons.'

'Are you warm enough, mother?' he asked when she had stopped laughing, his mouth dry, and she looked at him sharply, for the first time.

'The heat was tremendous,' she said, 'I couldn't possibly tell you, not like England. I went there once, when I was a little girl, I was so excited, they said just wait, you'll see so much, shops and churches and roads and, oh, I don't know what, all kinds of marvellous things, I was a little girl, I believed it, I didn't expect it to be so dark.'

She fell silent and his fear calmed. The television droned. The airless room made him sleepy. His mother began to talk again, and he thought of Giocattolo, those weeping pietas, records of a destroyed life, and when he woke half an hour had passed.

He cleared his throat and sat up. The two old women who had been asleep in front of the television had gone, and he was alone with his mother and the fish in their tank. His fear returned and he got up stiffly. 'I have to go now, mother,' he said. 'I'll see you next week. I'm glad you're looking so well.'

He cleared his throat again and thought that he would faint.

She looked up at him in confusion. 'Oh no,' she said. 'When I come here I don't pay, a long time ago I gave them fifty pounds and they said come back whenever you like.'

'Don't worry, mother, no one's asking you to pay.'

He would have said more but couldn't. He kissed her again and went, the taste of her hot skin in his mouth.

## III

Entering his living room, Mr Polunin saw her standing in front of the fireplace as if, with her neat blonde bob, white blouse (with a blue motif), severe pencil skirt, navy nylons and high-heeled shoes, she had just come home from the office to pose, emblematic of the transitory hour between work and home among the pools of lamplight and shadow which subdivided the spacious room. But she did not work, her clothes were always formal, and this was not her home. The blouse was frilled at the front and decorated with cross-stitches; her dress was too tight. Her bare arms were reflected in the mirror over the mantelpiece behind her. Mr Polunin shut the door, and stood there in the silence.

'You're late,' she said. 'I can't stay.' She must have let herself in with his spare key. Light from a lamp sparked the lenses of her glasses as she tilted her head to look at him sternly. After a minute he crossed the room.

For a while he struggled with her blouse, undoing some buttons with his fingers, some with his teeth. Snorting, he worked his mouth down her cleavage, spitting shirt cotton, lapping her skin and worrying her brassière with his pinched fingers. Echoes of his own noises sounded loudly in his ears. He was panting already and he thought briefly, for the second time that day, of his age. Through his shirt he felt her hand bump across the skin of his lower back; his jacket came off, falling to the floor, a shirt-tail flapped, and he heard her voice, a far-off sigh, in his ear. 'What?' he murmured loudly. His hand came up with a jerk clutching the hem of her blouse and he wrestled his fingers into the waistband of her skirt, feeling at the same time her leg rise like a ballerina's against his stomach, making him struggle to keep his balance as with one hand he pushed the rest of her blouse up her breasts and across her shoulders, and with the other took hold of the flesh of her hips, his fingers actually crushed, actually in pain. 'What?' he panted. 'What?' Her hands were raking his back, and his shirt was knotted up round his neck, obscuring his vision. His height played against him. Stooping and butting her with his face he wrapped his arms round her back and blindly sought the catch of her bra. 'Wait,' she was saying. 'What?' he said. 'Wait,' she said, but he continued to fight for purchase, breaking off every few seconds to run his hands up her ribs as if he had lost something, until, inserting them between the bra-strap and her back, he trapped them, and they were still. 'Wait,' she said loudly and broke free. His shirt fell from his neck, he opened his eyes and blinked. She unclipped the catch at the front of her bra, and stood breathing deeply with her hair in a mess, her bra, black lace decorated with red roses, hanging off her deeply-shadowed, mobile breasts, as he gawped, gulping for air or inspiration, then came onto her again hunched like a wrestler in an agony of awareness of his own strength. His face was craned into her mussed hair, and he could feel her hands on his shirtfront like pummelling fists as she tried to wrench open the buttons. 'Wait,' he said, but she succeeded in ripping an opening from the top, and he took his shirt and ripped the rest of it himself, panting and thrusting his chest against her breasts, crushing them, then drawing back and with a little cry scooping them up in his hands, like pets, as if undecided whether to throttle or resuscitate them, feeling them shift and bulge in his fingers. 'God,' he said. His belt was undone, her hands in his trousers, her arm cutting into his stomach. 'Wait,' he said, drawing her attention to his flies. She undid them, and his trousers fell, and they stood apart a moment getting their breath. 'What?' she said, and he pulled her against him and threw down the zip of her skirt which, inexplicably, he found at once, and dipped his head to kiss her throat, exploring her buttocks through her knickers, running his fingers under the elastic, pulling them slightly down, then slightly up, then slightly to each side in a rotary motion until, in an act of desperation or exasperation he pushed them down as far as her knees, lost them for an instant, then, locating them with his fingertips too far down to manipulate, attempted to drive them to her ankles with the sole of his foot which he raised like a heron, wobbling, clinging to her head for support, bringing his knee up into her breasts before realising that his trousers coiled round his ankles prevented the manoeuvre, and, staggering backwards, nearly dragged both of them to the floor. He moaned, and they separated. 'What?' she said. They cautiously crouched down and crawled away from the fireplace, trailing clothing, removing her knickers, the same black lace and red roses as the rest of it, some of it ripped where he had struggled with it. 'Here, here,' she said, impatiently pushing up her breasts to him, and he swayed forward and took a nipple between his teeth, hissing again, and began to work on the cuffs of her blouse. He was feeling very tired by now. Suddenly disengaging, she removed his legs from his trousers, and returned to his underpants and his swollen genitals. 'God!' he

said in his mild, refined voice. 'Oh God!' She strad-
dled his waist and squirmed, and he reared up as if
electrocuted and took the breast in his mouth again.
'Wait,' she said. 'Here. No, here!' He raised his hips
and she took hold of the waistband of his underpants
and fought for possession of them. They came off and
she worked them down his legs with her thighs, and
sat up again. 'Wait,' he said. 'This way.' He pushed
her round and went round himself in the other direction, using her shoulders, breasts, hips, buttock, as
handholds. 'Oh God!' she said, arching her back, as
she felt his tongue, or perhaps not his tongue, but his
mouth, his lips, and he took hold of her buttocks and
drew her against him again, trying to talk at the same
time and failing, and jerking his buttocks upwards as
if the carpet underneath him was red hot, as he felt
her lips, or perhaps tongue, on him. They were both
sweating now, he felt the sweat gathered in the crease
of her buttocks, and she felt the sweat on his matted
belly against her face. Grunting, he rotated again and
carried her partway with him and round until they
met and roughly synchronised with their heads now
at the lip of the fireplace, their legs interlocking. She
sat up and wiped her hair from her face, and he said,
'What?' 'Wait,' she said, and put one leg across his
midriff and the other round his neck and then the
first round his neck as well, and, grimacing under the
strain, he levered himself off the floor, and she frankly
reached down and took hold of his cock as if to steady
herself, and they both said together, 'Oh God!' The
strain was too much, and they knelt. 'Your shirt,'

she said. 'What, what did you say?' It hung from his wrists like a broken dancing partner, and they both struggled against it until the buttons popped and it fell off. He was naked now except for his argyle socks and grey shoes, and she had on one and a half stockings and a navy shoe, which, leaning forward, she removed. 'Wait now,' she said, and lay under him, and they fumbled together with their genitals, a common purpose dividing them until, like a cog clicking, it worked and their bellies met. 'Oh God!' he said. 'Wait!' she shouted. 'Wait!' 'Oh God!' he said again with a whimper, his back shuddering, and they moved against each other, dipping and shoving, avoiding their agonised expressions but pressing their faces into each other's throats and chests and hair as if trying to stifle sneezes, their bodies quaking with the effort. 'Oh God! Oh God!' he shouted, and she shouted, 'Wait!' and he felt somehow her knees at his chest, and then her legs over his shoulders, and his face bulged. 'Don't . . .' she said. 'Stop!' 'What?' he said, stopping. Her breasts shook under him. 'Don't stop!' she shouted, and he started again, and it was finally impossible to tell whose limbs were whose.

# A LONG TIME

On the first of March 1991 Jean Hurrell faced the facts about her physical appearance. It was her fifty-ninth birthday. The floods of February had finally receded, and she stood at her dining room window with a cup of coffee, looking out onto the wreckage of her garden.

As a young woman she had been ugly. In middle age she had been plain. Finally – and suddenly – she was beautiful. To her astonishment and regret, she found herself to be intensely attractive to men. Apparently the high point of a woman's sensual appeal, like moments of her greatest acuity, can happen at any age, old or young, impossible to predict, almost certainly dangerous. She did not like these facts, they disoriented her.

Self-images, formed in youth, are difficult to shake off. To think of herself as beautiful would be to mutilate the image which she carried in her mind. As a girl she had associated the sensation of being ugly with the urinous taste of asparagus to which she remained allergic, and to change her view of herself would be like eating it again.

Going upstairs to her bedroom, she looked at herself in the mirror. Her clothes were sensible and unfashionable, her hair orderly and neat, as it had always been. She took off her cardigan, blouse and skirt, and stood there in her underwear. Her breasts were heavy in the cups of her brassière. Her stomach, deeply creased at the navel, was solid and white over her knicker tops, and her legs were sturdy and dimpled. Her face, lifted into the light, seemed concentrated not in the eyes but in the mouth with its faint ring of grey hairs. Taken all together, she gave the unmistakable impression of sex. 'This is not me,' she thought. 'I am not desirable. I will not be desirable.' Ashamed of herself, she dressed in a shabby jumper and old corduroy trousers, went out into her garden and weeded the east-facing beds until she was tired.

Cherry blossom brightened the compost heap, the large chestnut tree at the end of the lawn (which she had planted as a girl) cast a shadow over the bright wet grass as far as the house. She could not escape Nature. Inexplicably, at an age when she might have been a grandmother, she had become what she most feared: an object of desire.

By six o'clock the sun had sunk, the sky was deep blue overhead and leaky pink beyond the terracotta Parkside roofs. The sunset was elsewhere, in the park. There the sky would be like the cracked gold background of a Sienese master, reflected in the dazzling lake, a blaze at the end of the day. As Jean Hurrell looked up, a child's silver balloon crossed the roof of her house and ascended steeply into the sky;

and at the same time the church bell began to ring for evensong.

She craved peace but her affliction gave her no rest.

Resting on her fork, she looked across neighbouring gardens and saw Mr Polunin making his way slowly to his shed where he kept his garden furniture. He was one of the longest-serving residents of Parkside Road, and, she guessed, about the same age as herself. His hair had been white for years, giving him an air, somehow, of inconstancy. They met occasionally at the museum where he was a visiting lecturer, and once she had had a crush on him, but had long ago decided he was homosexual. He moved slowly down his garden, very well-dressed, ignoring everything around him. Age had not made *him* more attractive, she decided.

Seeing Mr Polunin made her think of her own work at the museum. For thirty years she had been assistant curator of the antiquities collection. It was her life. The administration was mundane and never varied except in terms of its quantity which steadily increased, but her love of the objects she tended had never diminished. Every lunchtime she still went down to the cast museum in the basement and walked between the haphazardly arranged plaster replicas, a dense crowd of familiar, remote figures, no less beautiful for being scuffed and mutilated. Polyclitus' *Doryphorus*, *The Kritios Boy*, *Hippodamia Attacked by a Centaur*, *The Dying Niobid*, *Aphrodite of the Cnidians* – they had become as necessary to her as family.

Here, as nowhere else, she was at ease. Close to the figures, surrounded by them, circulating among them as in a complicated dance, she felt the same sensual light-headedness she had twenty years earlier as a young woman. Usually, at the end of her lunch break, she stood for five minutes in front of the three surviving versions of *The Wounded Amazon* attributed to Phidias, Polyclitus and Cresilas. A yellowed index card (which Jean Hurrell had typed herself in 1961 as a research assistant new to the gallery) stated that the figures were believed to be entries in a competition entered by the greatest of the Greek classical sculptors in the mid fifth century BC. Each competitor was required to sculpt the life-size figure of an Amazon wounded in battle, then judge the sculptures himself and put them in order of beauty. The winner – Polyclitus' version – was the work which each of the other sculptors had placed second to his own. Unfortunately no one now knew which of the surviving Amazons were by which sculptors. There was only opinion – which some argue is the whole of beauty. None of this had ever mattered to Jean Hurrell. The statues of the Amazons made her day lighter, and their deaths were a part of her life.

She shivered: the sky was dark and a wind had risen. A crow going silently past the end of the garden was an intermittent shadow against the line of lit bedroom windows in the houses opposite. In a few days she was going abroad, and when she got back, the primroses and pansies would be out. Each March, before the weather was too hot, she took a Swan Hellenic party to the Greek mainland and spent two weeks visiting sites with them and giving lectures in the evenings, returning home at the end of the month exhausted, sunburned and rapturous to a damp English spring and her garden in bloom. She had never looked forward to the trip so much as this year. This year it would be her escape.

The start of all her trouble, the discovery of her sex appeal a year earlier, seemed exemplary; she thought of it often, with a shudder. One evening a young man in his thirties, an authority on French illuminated manuscripts of the later medieval period, came to her house to borrow some catalogues. It was a stormy March evening, the trees in the park were wild, leaping and clashing inside their black outlines like animals in a cage. Down Parkside Road the tightly-knit lamplit housefronts streamed and the hedges shook. Raindrops burst against the windows. The young man came through to the kitchen and stood wiping his face with a towel and admiring Jean Hurrell's cats while she made mugs of coffee. Then they went into the lounge, a comfortable room full of old furniture and dim standard lamps trailing flex, and he began to look along the bookshelves. She had already sorted out the catalogues for him, they were in a pile on the table, but he leisurely looked along the bookshelves, talking about his favourite works of history. He admired the German tradition, he said, despite the fact that it was unfashionable. His beard, she noticed, was not quite clean. He had long hands and a nervous manner. She was wearing an old grey woollen skirt which for some time she had been meaning to take to the charity shop.

Suddenly, standing next to her as she held volume three of the *Cambridge Ancient History*, he put his hand on her left breast. They froze together, like a statue of a mythological scene, and he said, almost choking, 'I must be mad, but I want to make love to you.'

She threw him out.

But it was only the beginning. By the autumn a pattern had been established. Hardly a week went by without some approach being made. The attendants at the museum, all family men, took to staring at her. Her senior male colleagues found things which they needed to discuss with her over dinner. The director, previously indifferent to her, enquired in his vaguely camp manner whether she would care to attend the Society of Antiquarians' Annual Banquet with him. When they talked to her, these men shared an attitude which suggested daring sympathy, as though they forgave her for transgressing a minor social convention, like wearing shorts to work or riding a motorcycle. She bore it all with dignity, but in the evenings, as she cleared leaves in her garden, she was angry and fearful to think of her life changing beyond her control.

Scenarios had been hinted at. Furtive episodes in the museum, sluggish animation among the still forms of beauty and desire. Entertainments, dinner parties, fingers on her legs under the table. Trips abroad, first-class hotels, luxury, indulgence. Marriage, shared mortgages, adopted families and retirement cottages with walled gardens.

She had never thought of herself as an angry person, or even an emotional one, but now, as soon as she woke in the mornings, she felt her fury simmering inside her, and lay awake in bed, irritated by birdsong, the first cars of the commuters and the electric milk float. In the evenings she raked leaves. She made piles of them, took them to the compost heap and set them alight, burned them in a furious blaze, watched them flare and swirl, bending intently to shovel the flames.

But March had come at last, and her annual trip to Greece. Athens in March with its traffic jams, dust, noise and dirt had given her the most lyrical moments of her life; now it offered sanctuary.

It started badly. On the coach from the airport to the Hotel Dionyssos three different men − all widowers − sat next to her in turn and talked in a shared demotic of their private sorrows and personal qualities. In the hotel a squabble developed between a retired sales manager and a widowed librarian both of whom wished to escort her to dinner. Over the next few days it was the same, she was never safe from insistent, almost desperate intrusions, she could not even attempt a walk in the evening after her lecture was over without contentious offers of company. Each night she retired to her room distraught.

When she had free time she sought the tourist spots which the 'connoisseurs' of her Swan Hellenic party avoided. Three afternoons running, in pure desperation, she visited the Acropolis. Even so early in the season, it was crowded, a bomb site swarmed over by survivors. Distracted and unhappy, she circulated across the rubble with the rest, seeing herself strangely, as if her body were isolated from her past, like a Wounded Amazon, an object rejected by time and picked over by the mutilating crowds. She feared a breakdown.

It was her belief that there were only two kinds of person: happy and unhappy. When I was ugly, she thought, I was happy. Now I'm *changed* (she couldn't bring herself to describe her condition), I'm unhappy. I am now an unhappy person.

By five o'clock the crowds had dispersed, but she did not dare return to the hotel before dinner. Making her way off the hill, she loitered uncertainly in the strip of souvenir shops and restaurants below. Streets which in the tourist season bore so much humanity, so much emotion and weariness, shared neither in the purity of classical architecture nor the nostalgia of picturesque ruins; they had been made ugly by use and improvement. But she had had enough of beauty, she went into a café at the end of the street and ordered a mineral water.

The proprietor was a fat man with a crumpled face whose moustache wagged as he chewed. He stood behind the counter wiping cups with a towel, like a caricature of a Greek café proprietor. He did not even glance at Jean Hurrell when she spoke to him, but moved slowly to the fridge, fetched a bottle of mineral water and a glass, put them down on her table, and went back to wiping and chewing. His fingernails, she noticed, were dirty.

The café itself was dirty. Sipping her water, she looked at the curling postcards on the walls, and the litter on the floor, cigarette butts, torn sachets and bottle caps.

For an hour she sat with her water, close to tears. Once or twice she blew her nose. Eventually she got up to settle her bill, and the fat man, not looking up from the cup he was wiping, told her curtly that there was nothing to pay.

She said she did not understand. He shrugged and went on wiping.

'How much do I owe you?' she asked again, sharply, hearing the accent in her voice.

The Greek stopped wiping and glared at her. It seemed to be the first time he had looked at her. His eyes were moist and dark, his eyebrows darker. 'How much?' he said. Although she had spoken to him in Greek, he replied, angrily, in English. 'How much?' Inexplicably he was almost shouting. Controlling himself, he said, 'For some things — money; for others — no. You don't understand this simple thing?'

She demanded an explanation. He refused to give one, and she left with a gesture of contempt.

That night she slept badly, and the following day she could not stop thinking about the episode. After a year of condescension and insinuation from colleagues and friends this trivial but enigmatic rudeness from a total stranger moved her to passion. Her fury flared up in the heat. Late in the afternoon she returned to the café.

Again she was the only customer. The proprietor was still wiping cups with a towel, and she watched him while she drank her mineral water. He was heavier than she remembered, with unshaven jowls and a manner which would have been slothful if there had not been a nervousness in his hands and an expression of startled resentment in his eyes. He kept his head down, wiping cups and chewing slowly.

When she had finished her mineral water she went to the counter, put her money on it and stared defiantly at him. He swept it onto the floor, banged down the cup he was wiping and shouted, 'Yesterday I told you! You want to pay, go somewhere else, stay away from this place!'

'I insist you explain,' she demanded. 'I have never heard anything so insulting.' The prim Englishness of her voice shocked her.

'You think I am blind?' he said, and when he put his fingers to his eyes she saw his hands were trembling.

She looked at him amazed.

'You think what?' he said. 'That I think you come here because you like it?' He waved his arms round the room, gestures enormous and anarchic. 'That I think you like the postcards on my walls? The dirt on my floor? This? This? This?'

Spittle flecked his moustache and cheeks.

He shouted, 'You don't like the postcards! Trash, they are trash! You don't like the mineral water! It is the worst mineral water in the world! You don't like my café! This café, it is a mess, it is filthy, it is not beautiful!' He slapped his hands on the counter. 'What is it, you think I have no heart?'

But when she held his gaze – surprising herself with her determination – he subsided with helpless gestures and looked away and said quietly, 'I am not blind, I see you crying. So you come here because, I don't know why, because you have nowhere else to cry.'

For a second there was silence, and then, as if he feared for his reputation, he began to shout again, pacing behind his counter. 'So you are sad! What sadness? It doesn't matter. Sadness. It's not my business, I can't make your sadness go away. You try to pay! What am I to do? You want me to die a sinful man?' Turning on her heel, Jean Hurrell walked out, her eyes bright.

The next day she returned again and this time ordered two mineral waters. She had not known herself capable of such effrontery, she had forgotten both the harassment of the Swan Hellenic widowers and the beauties of classical Athens. The café proprietor looked at her, not knowing what to do. He snorted.

'I will burn in hell,' he said.

'You will go out of business,' she said, and laughed in his face. Again she felt very English standing there in a beige cotton blouse and skirt, hearing her own voice with its precise, nervous consonants. The proprietor went to the fridge, frowning like a sulky boy who has been found out.

His name was Andreos. The café had belonged to his parents, and he had worked in it since he was old enough to carry cups and plates. Most of the time he had hated it. When he was young he had wanted to be a chef, not a café cook like his father, but a master chef with his own restaurant. The money he earned from odd jobs went on cookbooks, he read the biographies of the great chefs and histories of gastronomy. Sometimes, when money was available, his father would bring him some fish or vegetables from the market, and after the café had closed in the evening, he would cook for the family, simple French dishes with complicated names he could not say, Fricassée Argenteuil, Vichyssoise, Bouillabaisse Provençale. When he talked about food his face lit up. He had dreamed of going to Paris and training under Albert Roux at Le Gavroche. For ten years he thought about nothing but opening his own restaurant. But he had never had the opportunity, and now his parents were dead. He was forty-five and too old to sell the café and start a different life. He did not even want to anymore. 'It takes a long time,' he said, 'to be yourself. You understand me? Now I am myself. I am my café. These postcards, this trash, this, this, this. This is me.'

'People lead such secret lives,' she said. 'Secret even from themselves.'

Andreos looked at her. 'I would like to cook a meal for you,' he declared.

For the rest of her stay in Greece Jean Hurrell saw no more art.

When she handed in her resignation at the museum,

the director asked to see her. He was solicitous and charming, touching her elbow as he drew her into his office. Through the window there was a sunlit view of the gables and drainpipes of the Victorian Gothic hotel standing opposite. After the February rain, he said, March had been a godsend. If there was anything she would miss, Jean Hurrell thought, it would be the drainpipes, the frankness of English plumbing.

He called to his secretary in the ante room to bring coffee and pastries, and then asked Jean Hurrell why, with only one year to retirement and a full pension, she was leaving. She told him. He laughed out loud. She repeated what she had said. His manner changed from levity to concern, then to incredulity, then from incredulity to annoyance. He disliked jokes. Rising from his chair he stood for some seconds with his back to her, looking out of the window. Then, warmly, he asked her to repeat what she had just said.

'I am going to Athens to marry a café proprietor fourteen years my junior.'

The director turned and looked at her for a long time, he seemed to be scrutinising her face for a flaw he might draw attention to. 'Even you,' he said at last. 'Even you can go too far.'

March was nearly over. On Sunday morning she walked in the park, thinking of nothing. On the lake the swans were mating, their necks entwined, beaks pointing to the sky, and the church bells were ringing as if they would never stop. Long ago she had ceased to think of Parkside as her neighbourhood, it had changed too much; but now, when it was too late, she had a sudden joyous sense of its residual habits and comforts. Sitting at the end of the boating pond, she smiled at it all, as if she had just come to consciousness on that park bench with only happy memories.

She left her house in Parkside Road in the hands of an estate agent, said goodbye to her cats and her garden, and flew to Athens. It was no good trying to anticipate the years ahead – the scalding summers with their locust swarms of tourists, the windy winters, the discomfort of Andreos's tiny flat above the café where they would live, the monochrome of dust, the blinding sky, the traffic, the piety, the cramped coolness of evenings – she could think of nothing but the present moment, and in that moment was all she wanted of happiness.

The years went by as if she were a new person and had started again, and then, at the beginning of the fourth summer, a routine medical check revealed traces of cancer in her liver. It is not uncommon in elderly women. The following week she was moved into the hospital. More sophisticated examinations showed the disease had already spread and she was not expected to live long.

Andreos shut the café and moved into hospital with her, preparing all her food and sleeping on a camp bed in her room. She was not surprised at the suddenness of events, nor even to be living in a hospital room;

she felt that she had become a person whose life was surprising in essence.

As she lay curved in bed, supported by pillows, her collar-bone starkly prominent above the neckline of her night-dress, she watched the sun setting over Mount Lycabettus, a brief radiance before night fell and the window brightened with the reflection of Andreos and herself in the bare white room. Her skin was bruised and hot and dry, and her breasts hurt when she moved so she lay as still as possible. Her face, as always, seemed concentrated in her mouth, in the lips, slightly apart to breathe more easily, and in the faint ring of grey hairs.

Andreos cooked for her with a desperation as if food might save her. Working in a corner of the hospital kitchen with borrowed pans and utensils, he prepared the French dishes he had cooked after hours in his parents' café as a boy. Each morning he searched the markets for the right ingredients, daikon for Miso Julienne, chervil for Fricassée Argenteuil; and in the evening he made soufflés and roulades, he poached and grilled fish, he marinaded lamb and fried chicken collops.

One evening she said to him, 'I wouldn't have let you cook Fricassée Argenteuil if I had realised what it was. I was forgetting that I used to be allergic to asparagus. But it doesn't seem to bother me now, I even liked it.' She was looking out of the window. The sun was setting, dusty orange. 'It takes a long time to be yourself,' she said, looking at him. 'But I have become someone who is not allergic to asparagus. At last!' Andreos went out of the room into the corridor so she would not see him crying and laughing at the same time.

Each day marked her deterioration. What was left of her hair was brushed back behind her ears. Her mouth was permanently open: she lacked the strength to close it. The grey hairs on her upper lip were distinct against her white skin. The short flounced sleeves of her night-dress showed the long bones of her white arms and the skin hanging off them. Her eyes, which had turned a cloudy yellow, never quite closed, even when she slept, though she saw nothing.

During the last few days she was delirious for long periods, and when her mind cleared she was left with memories of disconnected images, as if from a dream. Most of all she saw those cracked classical figures in the museum, especially the Wounded Amazons posed demurely in the basement, dying forever with quiet vivacity; and she thought that perhaps in the end all ways of dying are the same, her way no different from theirs.

Finally there was no more need to reflect: she was not alone with her memories, but part of them, as she was part of her tiredness. At her insistence her head was turned to face the window, even if she could no longer see it, and in the last hours her face with its tranquil expression of inward concentration was alternately lit with the lights from the blank blue, the sunset, and the reflection of herself and Andreos in the bare white room.

# MONKEY

Around mid-morning the gorilla suit got warm, and I stopped dancing and leaned against the side of the van and looked at the fair. What did Klee say? 'The artist does not reproduce the visible, rather he makes things visible.' I think of that sometimes.

The street had disappeared under the mass of people. Machinery hid the historic buildings, the street lamps were draped with flags. There was nothing to be seen of the road, no white lines, no bollards, no traffic lights. Instead there was the Fabulous Ferris Wheel, the Voyager, the Waltzer, the Merry-go-round, the Simulato; there were the catering mobiles, the balloon-sellers, the fortune-teller's tent, the St John's Ambulance booth. And there were the crowds of people wedged into the spaces in between.

Easter, coming in April, had coincided with the first real sun of the year. It was hot, as if not just spring but summer had arrived too. The men were wearing goatees, baggy denims with low-slung crotches and shirts like vast handkerchiefs; the girls were showing their navels, they wore tight faded jeans belted low round their hips, and white or pink or baby-blue cotton T-shirts which came down as far as the underhang of their breasts. All winter I look forward to the liberation of breasts. On the first warm day of the year breasts burst out everywhere, big and mobile inside thin T-shirts and flimsy blouses. As if a whole new sex emerged, like butterflies, in the sun.

At the edges of the crowd, watchful and shifty, the fair workers like myself gave out tickets and pocketed change. We were not part of the crowd, we were individuals, we stood apart and a little sullen: the thin dark man chain-smoking under a sign saying *Your Favourite Seafood* and the middle-aged blonde in the stretch pants taking money on the merry-go-round. The men looked mean and bored, the women joked and scowled. We stood ankle-deep in litter, deafened by rock music and the roar of the generators.

No one else was wearing a gorilla suit. I try to remember Kafka too. After horror, kindness, rage and scorn, there is only indifference. Not one person in a hundred looked at me twice.

For three days every Easter the city centre is taken over by the fair. I had forgotten it was coming until I saw a poster in the window of The Bird and Baby. *Want to work at the Funfair?* Something about the proposition, perhaps simply its surreal improbability, appealed to me. The thought of me, a so-called educated 'professional', even if a broken-down unemployed one, working machinery or collecting money alongside men with greased hair and tattoos and women with beautiful bodies and missing teeth, was tempting. I read the poster over my wife's shoulder, memorised it, and the following day went for an interview in another pub down the road, The Green Man. I told my wife I was having a drink with a friend. There are some things – many things – which it is not possible to tell my wife about. I love my wife, she is the most desirable woman I know, but I'm not able to talk to her.

Fifteen months ago my business – a two-man design agency – went bankrupt. It was Christmas 1993: I had just finished Cheever's *Letters* and was about to start Muriel Spark's *The Driver's Seat*. I have a theory about bankruptcy. Bankruptcy is an incurable condition. Like an attack of psoriasis, it happens late in life, for no discernible reason, and will not budge. There's a famous piece on bankrupts by the psoriatic American writer, John Updike. 'The bankrupt man dances . . . He spends money in restaurants and tips generously.' I don't recognise Updike's bankrupt man, however. He is confident, ostentatious and affluent; he dresses expensively and travels widely in connection with business generated by his bankruptcy. It must be different in America. Here I'm still stalling the creditors, the banks control my personal finances, and my house is double-mortgaged. I'm wearing a gorilla suit for twenty quid a day and lying to my wife.

I remember moving into Parkside: it was August 1988, house prices were just peaking. My wife took charge. By Christmas we had put in a loft conversion, extended the kitchen and begun a breakfast room. In the spring we redecorated everything twice. We bought a camper van, his- and her- wind-surfers, a thousand pounds worth of skiing equipment and a time share in Lanzarote. My wife has expensive tastes. I remember myself as I was then, almost as confident and as ambitious as her; I was in a beautiful phase, spending my money on clothes and haircuts. Now I am left with nothing but trite questions. And this is what I want to know: which is the real me? The one with the haircuts and clothes, or the one who dresses up as a monkey?

When I got to The Green Man I went upstairs to a room with bare plaster walls and floorboards, and waited twenty minutes to speak to a man called Mitch. I read Soren Kierkegaard's *Fear and Trembling*, the Penguin Classics edition with the sensitive pencil drawing of Kierkegaard on the front cover. In Kierkegaard I find both the power and fragility of defiance that I admire. When Mitch arrived he took me into another room across the landing and showed me a gorilla suit.

'What's this for?' I asked.

'Just see if it fits,' he said. His manner was irritable. 'I've had ten others already this morning, all of them too big. One of them was gorgeous, he had experience, talent. He had actual qualifications. But he was too big. If you take a small in gorilla suits you're a lucky bastard.'

'I thought I'd be operating machinery or taking money,' I said.

'Dancing,' he said. 'Dancing and giving out leaflets. Gus the Gorilla. It's the horror man's idea. Do you want the job or not?'

The gorilla suit fitted me perfectly.

Mitch led me back to the first room, and made me lumber up and down, grunting while he watched critically. 'Jesus,' he said. 'Do the beating your chest bit again.' Grumbling, he decided to give me a break. 'It's your lucky day, I can't afford to be choosy. Seven thirty, St Stephen's, you know where. Ask for the horror man.'

How can I describe the experience of wearing a gorilla suit? I wasn't embarrassed, but I felt different, childlike almost, as if, hiding from others inside a suit, I understood them less but watched them more, absorbed in everything behind staring eyes. I can't explain. Klee could explain. It was as if I looked at them so hard I invented them. I was frightened and gleeful at the same time.

There's a brief conversation in Hemingway's *The Sun Also Rises* which I read recently: '"How did you go bankrupt?" Bill asked. "Two ways," Mike said. "Gradually and then suddenly."' That's what I like, fragility and defiance.

The horror man employed two stooges. I was one; the other was a girl called Vicky who wore a fairy-tale princess's dress of cream nylon with silver brocade down the front. It was her job to clasp her hands together and shriek, my job to cavort round her. Occasionally we danced. I was happy to dance with her. She had told the horror man she wanted to go into the theatre, but he had obviously chosen her because of her breasts. Her breasts were dramatic.

We hadn't been working long when the sun came out, and the horror man, who sat in a booth behind us operating the rides, began to shout into a microphone to attract passers-by. 'Guaranteed terror, ladies and gentlemen! One hundred and ten per cent mind-boggling horror! You'll not sleep for a week!' Occasionally he would roar with laughter. It was a very off-putting performance. Trade was poor.

I began to sweat inside my acrylic fur. While the horror man shouted, I lurched along the narrow ledge in front of the van, grunting and beating my chest, sometimes dancing. I could not keep this up for very long. I am thirty-four years old and take no exercise. How could I have known that being a gorilla would be so demanding? But whenever I stopped to rest the horror man shouted into the microphone, 'Scared my chimp half to death, ladies and gentlemen! Poor bugger's on his last legs, see the show that terrified King Kong!'

The horror show was not well-placed in the fair, it was stuck on a narrow corner between the first aid centre and the Oxfam mobile. Most people passed without stopping, on their way to the Ferris wheel or the various merry-go-rounds. Those who did stop were waiting to meet someone. But I suppose the horror man had to blame someone. Just as I was slipping round the back of the equipment to take a rest (I had left a bottle of water and a new book in a bag by the generator) he came out of his booth to talk to me. He was a huge man with great blue cheeks, a speckled nose and wet hair.

'Listen to me,' he said. His voice, when not magnified

by the microphone, was high-pitched and thin. 'I want you to keep moving, I'm paying you to move. You're the worst fucking gorilla I've ever had. Frightening? You're more like Snot the dog than King Kong. Get frightening. Nod if you understand.'

When I had finished nodding Vicky and I danced up and down our ledge again, the beautiful and the ferocious, jigging down the steps to the street and dancing alongside passers-by who smiled and ignored our leaflets and hurried on. Teenagers sitting in the road smoked and jeered. Their hair was cut in a style I did not know the name of, the top half long and the bottom half shaved, as if they had been prepared for surgery. They had seen the horror man telling me off and began to taunt me. One boy in particular infuriated me. He had a milky young face and old expression, and stood with his arm possessively round a bare-naveled girl with glossy brown hair, and flicked cigarette ash down her front as he pointed and made gestures and told jokes. Everyone was screaming with laughter. I was so furious I wanted to go over and slap the cigarette out of his face, but I couldn't, perhaps I was afraid. Instead I held Vicky by the wrists (her eyes widening with surprise), and twirled her in a fast circle, grunting at the top of my voice. I couldn't stop myself. When we stopped, the boy and his friends had gone, there was nothing else I could do. My wife would say that I have trouble expressing my anger, but I say that when you are in a monkey suit you are a monkey. Sometimes, I admit, you don't need to put on a suit.

★    ★    ★

There was plenty of time to think while I was being a gorilla. Mostly I thought about myself. I am the only unemployed resident in Parkside: this is often the subject of the conversations I have with my wife. It is no exaggeration to say that I am obsessed with my wife, I think of her constantly. We sit in our unfinished – never-to-be-finished – breakfast room discussing my unemployment and related problems such as my anti-social reading habits, my inability to motivate myself, my unwillingness to voice enthusiasm or regret for our many home improvements (now abandoned), my reluctance to challenge the boys in the next street who my wife thinks may be responsible for damage to our car last autumn. This sounds as if my wife is critical, but she understands me, I am anti-social, unmotivated, cowardly and unenthusiastic.

'I love you,' she says. 'I want to help you, but think of our problems, Michael, think of the mess we're in.' My wife is a beautiful woman, she is tender as well as tough, she leans towards me and strokes my arm. Hair falls across her face. She has this massive softness which overpowers me, I can't explain it, it's like being drugged.

'I should have studied literature,' I say, 'not graphics. I should have read more books. I should have been a teacher not a designer.'

Late evening will find me in the garden doing a job, burning rubbish or shifting rubble. My wife will have reminded me about it. The sun falls quickly into the roof of the church but the sunset is elsewhere, on the other side of the park, and the air turns grey, then mauve, then charcoal. In the park the pale tassels which the willows drip into the lake will be shot with gold, the Roman candle blossoms of the chestnuts will glow, even the cow parsley along the path by the old vicarage will be lit with the sunset. But here in the back gardens colours leak from flowers, leaving them grey. Lights come on in back rooms up the street, illuminating tiny vistas of bedrooms, conservatories and extensions. Why are these lights always the same shade of peachy orange? Is it an effect of the dusk, or of the window-panes, or of the nostalgia that seems to pervade the twilight, as you stand in your garden, wishing you were different – younger or better or simply someone else? There are days when I hate Parkside, loathe the tidy flower beds, the sweet sound of the choir practising in the church. There are days when I love my bankruptcy, my abandoned home improvements, my debts, when I think that I am what all the other Parkside residents fear becoming. The alcoholic accountant, the beautiful redhead, the kindly lady with the chic hair, 'the boys', the supercilious doctor, even the supercilious doctor's children – all of them in their time have looked at me and trembled. I am their nemesis, the absurd failure at the end of the street. I could laugh, and Klee and Kierkagaard would laugh with me.

Not for long, of course. Odd moments won from the general gloom.

Being a gorilla was arduous work. By lunchtime I was dancing as slowly as I could, to conserve energy. It was very hot. Inside my suit sweat trickled down my face, back and legs. Vicky was still fresh. She was young. Passing boys directed a lot of comment at her, and she played up to it, wringing her hands and squealing, 'Help! Help! Won't somebody please rescue me? I'm in quite a lot of danger!' I suppose I suffered by comparison. The horror man was shouting, 'Step right up ladies and gentlemen, see Princess Strudel the buxom beauty and Godzilla the beast with teeth the size of tent pegs and a brain the size of a pea!' That got quite a lot of laughs, if no customers. I stirred myself to make an extra effort – but then a terrible and unexpected thing happened. As I lumbered along the walkway towards Vicky I suddenly saw my wife and my son and my wife's mother coming towards me through the crowd, my wife pushing the buggy, her mother with her coat on despite the heat, two-year-old Harvey toddling alongside behind a raised clump of candy floss. I stopped, not quite believing it. Then, a second later when I did, I lost my head and was pushing past Vicky to hide when she, misunderstanding my intention, caught me by the waist and began to shout to my family, who had drawn level, 'Help, I'm being molested, I'm being molested, please help, *please!*' Unlike all the other passers-by, they stopped and stared. It was a terrible shock. I had my arms round Vicky. My wife looked very beautiful, she's had her hair done in a neat bob and has bought a number of expensive new clothes. I love her for her defiance. She was wearing a tight navy pencil skirt, very elegant, and a white blouse with a sort of blue motif across the front, frilled and decorated with cross-stitches. We stared at each other and I let go of Vicky and had started to mumble an apology, an explanation, before I remembered that I was in disguise. I relaxed, or, at least, froze.

I had told my wife that I was going to an interview for a job on a newspaper in another city. For a second I worried that she would go to the job centre and find out I was lying. But this was unlikely. There were carrier bags piled in the buggy; I remembered that she had planned a day's shopping.

Harvey was staring at me. Or rather he was staring at the gorilla. I wish the horror man had seen his reaction, he might not have complained. Harvey made a perfect face of terror, a sort of cartoon, and screamed so loudly he dropped his candy floss. With a speed I rarely credit her with, my wife swept him up with one arm, and her mother picked up the candy floss. He peered at me over my wife's shoulder, his eyes enormous, and I stared back, hairy arms dangling at my sides.

'It's alright,' my wife was saying to him. 'It's just a stupid man in a costume, don't be frightened. Look, it's not real.' My wife and her mother came towards me, their arms pointing, their reassuring faces turned towards my son, who did not take his eyes off me.

There have been moments in my life when something seems suddenly wrong, moments as sharp as a slap. I actually look around to see what has happened, and see that nothing has changed at all, except myself.

It has happened to me a few times since the bankruptcy, and it happened now.

'It's funny, isn't it?' my wife was saying to Harvey. 'Isn't it funny? What a funny thing!' Her false smile was enormous, I could see her gums. 'A funny man dressed like a monkey.' She chuckled. Had I ever heard my wife chuckle before? It was the most appalling noise in the world, it sounded like a life coming to an end.

I panicked and began to dance, slowly at first. Harvey screamed and I froze again. We looked at each other: he looked at me from behind my wife's shoulder, I looked at him from inside my monkey mask. Neither of us was sure of the other.

What I was thinking was this: Harvey is not my natural son. When I'm unhappy I often think this. It's true, and it isn't true. What I mean is, my wife and I couldn't have children on our own, we needed medical help. The IVF treatment lasted several years. We swore to each other that it would never lessen our joy in our son, that on the contrary it would increase it; but it is difficult sometimes even to be calm. For instance, we can't forget the stupid fact that he cost us several thousand pounds, one of our many debts. It is surprisingly hard not to think of this. These were the thoughts that went through my mind as I stood in the road in a gorilla suit, my son in a state of terror in front of me.

He looked at me. I made a bow, and when I looked up he was smiling, and my wife was smiling with him. It was like a miracle. Giving a small cry myself –

another grunt to him – I swung my arms slowly from the elbows, and walked in a small circle with my knees bent. He was no longer frightened, he was laughing. My wife was laughing, and her mother too. Inside my mask I could feel my face twisting.

'Meet other terrifying beasts inside!' the horror man shouted. 'Fun for the kiddies. Shake hands with Godzilla! Swap jokes with Frankenstein!'

They were going, Harvey holding onto his grand-mother's hand, looking back towards me, his big head wagging on his thin neck, a pink smear of floss on his chin. He was disappearing into the crowd. If only I could take my mask off and run after him, if only I could swing him up into my arms and tell him what it means to be his father. But the horror man was shouting, and I had to stay and dance.

There's a line in Shakespeare which I forget, but it's true, we're not what we seem; we're men changed into monkeys, or monkeys changed into men. We're strangers to ourselves.

I had a quarter of an hour for lunch, enough time to grab something from Burger Heaven. I didn't want longer, I felt exposed and unsettled with my mask off, a hybrid with a monkey's body and a man's head. There are worse mutations, I suppose.

While I ate I watched the crowd. Overhead, the swaying seats of the Fabulous Ferris Wheel shunted through oily sunlight, the Simulator shuddered on its pod. I could smell the fair for the first time – burgers, candy floss and diesel. Gradually I relaxed.

As I watched, a girl in a blue white-spotted dress won a genuine Garfield from the hoopla. With both hands she clutched her girlfriend's arm and squealed; and her short dress which was flared from a tight waist flipped up to show most of her legs. She seemed young; I couldn't be sure she didn't have a ribbon in her hair. Watching her, I tried to imagine my wife wearing the dress, a ribbon in my wife's hair. All the time I ate I was watching the girl. She had a habit of running her hand through her hair, pushing it around her head, as if trying to disguise herself, as if afraid, even as she laughed with her friend, of being recognised.

The best poem on lust that I know begins: 'Filling her compact and delicious body/ with chicken paprika, she glanced at me/ twice./ Fainting with interest, I hungered back/ and only the fact of her husband and four other people/ kept me from springing on her.' John Berryman wrote it, another American. What is it about America that they can be so frank about these things? Lust is one of the great themes, I think. There are too many bad books, and not enough good ones, about lust.

The girl in the blue white-spotted dress had disappeared. That's the way they go, appearing suddenly and melting away, leaving you to torment yourself with the thought that you will never see them again. In less than an hour even the memory of them is gone. Though you try so hard to fix them in your mind the details vanish – the extraordinary colour of their hair, the surprising shape of their faces, the astonishing beauty of their postures; things to heal and uplift, gone.

★   ★   ★

In the afternoon the sun was fiercer, my gorilla suit damper. I was very bored and pensive. I think the heat made me slightly delirious.

I danced, I beat my chest, I cavorted round Vicky who stood on tiptoe and preached her chastity, I slouched along my ledge, I crouched in the road and let my hairy knuckles trail on the asphalt, I swung from imaginary creepers, I grunted till I was hoarse. I don't know what I did, there were a thousand variations and there were none, time dragged and went by in an instant.

By three o'clock I was exhausted. Not caring what the horror man might say, I went round the back of the van for a rest, thinking of my bottle of water and new book, and came across a boy and girl wedged between the generator and trailer. Her dress was rucked round her waist and his trousers were undone. I stared. It was the boy with the milky face and old expression – but the girl was not the one with glossy brown hair, she was a blonde with a snub nose. I groaned, though all they would have heard was a grunt. The boy just glanced at me, and carried on mechanically, and I turned immediately and went; just the sight of them left me exhausted. It seemed to knock all my energy out of me. After the ups and downs of the day all that was left was Kafka's indifference.

Back on my ledge I trailed up and down, as apathetic as a gorilla in a zoo, irritably dreaming. It was my low point as a monkey. I couldn't stop myself thinking of all the things that had happened that day. I thought of the school boy with his pre-surgery haircut and two girlfriends, of the girl in the blue white-spotted dress, of my son traumatised by the sight of me, of my beautiful wife in her beautiful clothes. These were the things I had made visible. I suppose I was disgusted with myself.

For the rest of the afternoon I was nauseous and listless. I regretted being a monkey, even for a day. Vicky left early to see a film, and the horror man all but gave up his patter. Evening fell. The crowds thinned. At closing-time the horror man turned off the music, climbed out of his booth and, without saying a word, or even looking at me, walked off towards The Bird and Baby. All over the fair they were turning off the music and shutting down the generators. Genteel city noises of slow traffic crept back, flat and empty after the vulgar din of music and generators. The road reappeared, covered with litter.

As the lights went off, the street turned grey and yellow, and the sky seemed to appear again above it, a mottled wet purple. Mitch came over and gave me a broom and some plastic sacks.

'When you've finished, come for your pay packet to The Green Man,' he said. He looked at me while I stood with the broom and sacks. 'The horror man's not pleased,' he added. 'Not pleased at all.' He was about to add something, but someone called him, and he left.

The last people were drifting away, dragging their

children. Birds waddled on the road picking through the litter, and there was a dead crow lying in the gutter like a broken toy. I thought of my wife, I pictured her sitting in our unfinished breakfast room looking at me and lifting hair from her beautiful face, talking, as if she were in the middle of a conversation about me which would go on for ever.

How much I must have wanted to hurt her to take the job as a monkey at a fair.

People went past, going home, and I stood there with my broom and bin liners, not moving. Among them, suddenly, was the girl in the blue white-spotted dress. I was staring at her before I realised who she was. She was standing close by, resting her Garfield on her hip like a baby, eating a stick of pink rock and talking to her girlfriend. She was knock-kneed, I realised. When she giggled I could see her brace. She was no older than sixteen.

Her friend pointed, and they gawped.

'Didn't know there was a zoo round here,' the girl-friend said, and they giggled together. 'Did you know that, Garfield?' she said. Giggling, hardly looking at me, they made comments about me to Garfield, about my ugliness, my diet, my virility.

After a minute I took a step towards them, and they took fright like birds, hopping backwards, waving their arms. Another step, and they were backed up against Burger Heaven, weak with laughter. My legs were trembling too, but they still didn't look at me, their glances darted away, embarrassed and sly. After a pause I made a bow. They oohed and giggled, and the girlfriend took hold of Garfield's front paws and made him clap. At the other side of the fair there was one sound system still going, its music faint and out of place, and I began to dance to the rhythm, slowly at first, as I had for my son, then quicker and looser, rolling at the hip, letting my arms dangle at the elbow. They oohed again, grew bolder and applauded. I grew bolder in turn and changed tack, dancing smoothly, human-like, closer towards them. Her girlfriend pushed the girl in the spotted dress forward and I caught hold of her hand.

'Ooh, it's hairy,' she shouted back to her friend. Then I was spinning her, dancing on my hairy toes, grunting softly. All thoughts, all images of the day vanished, I forgot everything that had happened to me while I was in the gorilla suit. Nothing was in my mind as we danced through the litter piled at the side of Burger Heaven. I seemed hardly to exist, I was responsible only for moving the gorilla suit this way and that. It was a moment won from gloom which might dissolve at any time, it would have only taken the schoolboy with one of his girlfriends to come walking past and see me, but although I half-looked for him he did not come. The girl in the blue white-spotted dress danced closer and faster, and she held onto me as we span, laughing; and as she laughed, the flare of her dress flying, I put my paw down and touched her leg, and she squealed with surprise and laughter, and turned to see if her friend had seen, but kept dancing and holding me, and said, in a voice both stern and flirtatious, 'You *are* a monkey, you are!'

# MAY '96

## Wednesday 1 May

Warm today. Smells in the park of cut grass and tar.

Woken twice in the night: 1.47 (Tomos: change), 4.43 (Rhian: wet bed). The digital bedside clock fixes the interruptions in time like record-book statistics.

## Thursday 2 May

Warm again. Describe the street. Cow parsley in the hedgerows. Copper beeches light maroon (later they will turn almost black, out of love, out of pure grief). Extraordinary number of insects. Noise of a passing train like a downpour.

Woken twice: 3.03 (Rhian: nightmare), 4.11 (Tomos: feed). I sat on Simon's side of the bed with Tomos on my lap like a cat and watched the yellow lamplight through the curtains. The big wet kiss of his mouth on me. As I listened I heard the train again fading to the near-silence of half-imaginary sounds, Tomos breathing, Simon grinding his teeth in his sleep. A part of me recognised this as peace, but I was too tired and desperate for sleep to feel peaceful.

*Friday 3 May*

Drizzle making me nostalgic for school: head girl dreaming of a lifetime of responsibility. Five For Sale signs in the street. Making phone calls all day about an unpaid electricity bill.

Friday night the worst night this week. First woken at 1.06: Tomos screaming. 1.30 changed him, 1.45 fed him, 2.00 walked him. At 2.15 he came into our bed, and Simon went downstairs to the sofa. The warmth and small chunkiness of him, the hot mop of his hair, his fists clenching and unclenching. At 3.15 Simon came back, stayed for half an hour, and went again: the farce of bed-swapping. Tomos and I tried to sleep; he woke every half hour until 5.30, and at 6.00 Rhian got up and the day began.

I am astonished at myself, my powers of endurance. I am used to early morning light-headedness, mid-morning nausea, lunchtime anxiety, afternoon lethargy, evening panic. My great subjects, in fact.

Simon going off to work, bitter and childish. 'This is the Age of Frenzy', etc. Row at breakfast. For a second, in my tiredness, I think it is perfectly plausible that I am the most suffering person in the world. In the whole street.

*Saturday 4 May*

In the evening, as Rhian was going to the toilet just before bed, she said, 'Why mustn't you rip string, Mami?' 'What do you mean, darling?' 'Why mustn't you rip it?' 'You mean cut it, like in the Winnie-the-Pooh story where . . .' 'No, Mami, *rip* it.' '*Rip* it? I don't understand, darling.' 'I'm talking about string! String in different countries, different types of string, different *phases* of string!' 'Did you say "skin"?' '*String*, Mami! Why won't you *listen*?' Her tone is mine. But where does she get the words? I'm proud of her, but I wish the words were Welsh. In my own children, this dying out of my own language.

*Monday 6 May*
On the way back from nursery met the blonde woman from down the road, with her boy, Harvey. Describe her. Her name is Linda Ainsling. We have lived in the same street for years and never talked until now. She has a dishevelled husband with a yellow beard. Harvey is three and has just started at the nursery, like Rhian.

'What a pretty girl,' she said. 'What a handsome little boy. Tell me, where do you have your hair done?' She is thirty-four years old, has a well-educated voice and an immaculate blonde bob. When she talks she looks about her, as if hoping to catch sight of someone she knows, or for someone she knows to catch sight of her. She does not work. She is aware, above all, of her good looks; she shops — I guess — at Whistles and Oasis. So I add her to my catalogue.

*Wednesday 8 May*
At nights, the fear of burglars on me, I wish we still had a dog. Only Saturday I thought this. Then, last night, about ten, we were disturbed by the big blond South African we call Mr Nosey shouting, 'Burglar,

burglar, call the police!' Great panic, all the lights going on. 'He's in the gardens!' Mr Nosey shouting. Noises of trampling in the bushes. 'Call the police for God's sake, call the police!' Noise of Mr Nosey in pursuit of burglar, trampling through the bushes, shouting, 'You bastard! You bastard!' and appealing for help: 'Call the police for God's sake, will you call the police!' 'Alright, alright,' I heard someone grumble, 'I'm doing it, stop going on.' The noises died away. Neighbours stood in their gardens talking over the fences or gazing into the bushes in the allotment at the back, and after a while Mr Nosey returned via the road, puffing, and went straight into his house. A police helicopter passed overhead a few times, then silence. This morning Linda Ainsling told me that Mr Nosey ran into Wether Road and violently accosted a man out walking his dog. 'Bloody idiot,' Simon says. Since he got the consultancy and research job he wastes no opportunity to agitate for us to move house. 'All I want is a place where we can have some ordinary peace, etc.'

Twice in the night his bleeper went. First it woke Rhian, then Tomos.

*Thursday 9 May*
Birds on the lake. Mallards laughing at dirty jokes, arf–arf. Coots making noises like squeaky gates.

Woken three times: 12.48 (Huw: nightmare), 3 something (Tomos: feed), 4.30 (Tomos: feed). Statistics are like little pins I stick into my skin. I wonder why I'm not ill. Am I ill?

*Friday 10 May*

Went from the nursery to Linda's for lunch. Their house is half over-decorated, half unfinished – very odd. A scheme of turquoise and magenta in the front room. It took ten minutes for Harvey and Rhian to fight, and after that they played in separate corners of the room, and it was peaceful. Rhian saying, every so often, 'Mami, I want to go now.' Linda put on a video which I tried hard not to think inappropriate.

Her husband appeared and went again. Describe him. Michael is his name. He does not speak. He is a designer but apparently he sold his business just before the recession and does not need to work. 'He does nothing but read all day,' Linda said. Odd having half the house undecorated. Questions prick at me. Why are they living in this street? Why are they together? The questions remind me of the notebooks I used to keep when I was a student, and thought I was smart.

*Saturday 11 May*

Huw at a party in the afternoon. He came home late, very excitable, causing great delay and confusion. Eventually all the children in bed by 10. At 10.30 we heard strange noises from upstairs. Rhian had climbed out of bed and, unable to turn the stiff door handle, was lying with her face on the carpet next to the bedroom door, shouting hoarsely under it, 'Breakfast! Breakfast!' In the confusion we had forgotten to give her tea.

Woken three times: 1.00 (Tomos screaming), 1.46

(Tomos screaming), 5.10 (Rhian: wet bed). Now, whenever I think of Tomos, I think not of a boy with dimples and hot hair but fifteen months of sleeplessness. Nothing works. Simon says it's normal. 'It's normal hell,' he says. 'It's what people are, even your own children. Why did we have them? Why did we have so many, so soon, etc.' His accusing look.

*Sunday 12 May*
In the park. The model boat enthusiasts with their battleships, frigates, gun-boats – all elderly – intently circling the pond, as if on real manoeuvres. Rhian confided in me that she could see much better in the dark than she could in daylight. 'Do you know, Mami? In the day, I haven't got the light in my eyes. Not like you,' she added, after some thought. When we reached the vicarage she developed another theory: she has a camera in her head. 'When I do this,' she said (rubbing the side of her right eye with her right forefinger), 'it takes a photograph. It goes into my ear, and then I can take another photograph.' Moving her hands as she explained, wiggling them round. I am so proud of her. I couldn't have held her back with Welsh – but a part of me suffers.

Saw Linda and Harvey in the park. Harvey was building a pile of woodchips under the climbing frame, Linda sitting on a bench twenty yards away, staring towards the line of cypresses. I waved, but though she was looking my way she seemed not to see me.

*Monday 13 May*

Linda and Harvey for tea. As if by agreement Harvey and Rhian ignored each other from the beginning: very peaceful. Linda complained about the neighbourhood: how expensive the corner shop is, how ugly and forbidding the church, how unfriendly people are. Seeming not to be aware that this implicated me. Her make-up was heavy, her finger-nails glossy and bitten. At school she would have moved in dangerous circles, she would have been knowledgeable about drink, boys, cigarettes. I can imagine myself a younger girl, overhearing her laconic conversations about heavy emotions, never daring to speak to her.

Woken in the night, I lost count of the number of times. As if this were not enough, Simon's bleeper went twice as well. Describe it. The house cold. Electric light hurting my eyes. A memory of Rhian running naked along the hall, and me stumbling after. Her girly bum. My sudden fear I would faint, fall on top of her. These fainting auras are common now; they rarely lead to a faint, but I often feel ill. Sometimes my mind seems to be working wrong.

*Wednesday 15 May*

Funny thing last night. At midnight there was a knock on the door. Simon went down, cursing, in an old jumper and mud-stained track suit bottoms, and a minute later came up and sent me down. Linda Ainsling was on the doorstep, furious. 'He forgot,' she said. 'Typical of him.' Spitting out the

141

words. 'Simon?' I asked, shocked. It seemed perfectly possible to me that this strange woman should criticise my husband (and I wonder, in fact, whether I would have defended him). 'No,' she said. 'Michael.' She said no more, but looked about, distracted. 'What did he forget?' I asked. 'To invite you to dinner,' she snapped. She was so emotional, my first thought was she must mean the dinner was to have been that evening, now obviously ruined, and I began to sympathise. 'No,' she said, impatiently, as if I were dim. 'A week on Saturday.' *A week on Saturday?* Is she deranged? Why wake us up at midnight to tell us this? 'That's fine,' I said. She seemed astonished by this, and obscurely angry with me. Both of us were now astonished. Reluctant to leave, she stood in the pathway looking at me, alternately smiling and frowning, until suddenly she recovered her poise, and said briskly, 'About eight. *If* you can make it.' She was beautifully dressed in a dark blue pullover and dark blue skirt. The skirt was rather tight, but she has a good figure. She has presence. For the first time I imagined her in the drama of sex; I have the impression she does not like it.

Bad night.

I used to want to write. The strangeness of that now. Now I am reduced to this diary, the last little compulsion. Nothing but a bald record of suffering. (But if I stopped I would cease to be me.)

*Thursday 16 May*
Dusk. Sitting in the back room. The shower has

stopped, and if I went outside I would smell earth, plants. But I stay in this airless room, looking out through glass, listening to Simon losing his temper with the children downstairs. I won't think of that. What will I think of?

The sky. Describe it. It is full of drizzle, a pastel shade of grey, very refined. Everything takes its cue from it, acquiescing, becoming muted, grey, dull. One roof is shiny, all the others are matt. The colours of flowers leaking. Neat thin strips of Parkside gardens melting together. One street lamp, bright amber; one bedroom window that irresistible peachy orange of lit windows. We think other people's lives are irresistible so we think their windows are this irresistible colour. A sad theory.

This — this bit of journal — is what I am now. The rest is family. Is that what I think? I think some odd things, I think that the family has conspired to prevent me having a life of the mind, but it is very odd, I never wanted a life of the mind before. Now I do. I want to learn languages, I want to study history and moral philosophy. The Enlightenment interests me, and current architectural theory, and classical civilisation. I want to read Barthes and Walter Benjamin and Derrida, and Babel, Perec, Ruskin and Henry James. I want their dignified lucidity. I want to lose myself in them.

Last night Tomos screamed from 2 till 4. Simon and I went in in turns: after five minutes, ten, fifteen, twenty, etc. Enraged by our visits, he thrashed and screamed. Simon was hysterical by 2.15. 'Poisonous little bastard, doing it on purpose, etc.' Going in, hissing, 'Shut up, will you shut up,' etc., shaking the cot. Row in bed. His inarticulate fury. Then he got dressed and went out, slamming the door. I looked at the clock and it was 2.30. I lay there in Tomos's noise. I could not believe it was my fault, but the feeling of it grew and I fought it, and ended crying. When Simon came back it was 4.30 and I was still awake. He had hurt his leg falling on the tow-path near the ring road.

Laughable. I would call the doctor, but Simon is the doctor.

Even this diary makes me frightened. I imagine, after my death, people reading it and saying, Yes, this is where she went wrong, this is where the trouble started.

*Friday 17 May*
Perhaps I really am ill. The feeling comes over me sometimes that I am floating free of it all. Tomos crying all day. Though he is hungry and tired he won't eat or sleep. When I put him down (doing the washing up, making the lunch he won't eat), he begins to cry, he keels slowly forward like a sinking ship, mouth wide open and eyes scrunched shut, he lies face-down on the floor and sobs. He is so unrealistic, I want to kick him as he lies there. That's the kind of mother I have become.

Janine came this morning and spent two hours telling me, despite my obvious uninterest, that she found some 'female undies' in Mr Polunin's house. 'Jesus, this neighbourhood!' as Simon says. She described them minutely – black lace decorated with red roses – and capped the description by saying they were torn, 'as if someone had been pulling at them with his fingers or *his teeth*'. The poor girl is repressed. She says the strangest things. What use does she think I have for such information? She believes they belong to Mary Worral whom she dislikes. 'I know all the undies in this street, and since Mary came back, etc.'

This street! Layer upon layer upon layer. Under the banality the drama, and under the drama more banality, and so on, until I blow up. I hate living in a foreign country, most of all in England.

In the afternoon Linda came round without Harvey and stayed till dinner, praising my clothes, the house, my children, my husband. 'Where *did* you buy your shirt?' She made a sherry last an hour and a half. 'If I had another, I don't think I could stop.' She was tense, with a forced gaiety. Her brightness produced an atmosphere of expectancy, as if everything were leading up to some very important question, which she couldn't, in the end, bring herself to ask. The skin at the corners of her eyes, I noticed, is finely cracked as if wearing out with so much use. I imagined her in an elegant night-dress crying luxuriously in bed.

Woken twice.

Headache.

I think: if I could only talk to someone.

*Saturday 18 May*
Days of no time. Nothing that is not children and

sleep and lack of sleep. Tiredness, headaches, strange tastes in my mouth. Perhaps I really am ill.

Went to town with Rhian and Tomos, pushing them together, Tomos in the pushchair, Rhian riding shotgun. Saw the lake in the park through the trees at the end of the street, like a glimpse of sea, brisk and uplifting, and for a second I thought *It's all going to be alright*. We walked down Vicarage Lane and along Atwell Street. For something to say to the children, I described my headache. 'As if,' I said, 'there are two broken plates inside my head, their jagged edges grinding together.' Rhian, after some thought, asked, 'Is it mystraucordia?' Pronounced mice-straw-cordia, sounding plausibly – and incredibly – medical. 'What?' 'Mystraucordia.' 'I don't know what you're talking about. Does it have anything to do with mice?' 'Oh, yes. Mice mixed up with cats.' '*Mice mixed up with cats?*' She thought about this. 'Well, *one* cat.'

*Sunday 19 May*
Swallows, quite high, their flight a mix of agitated bursts and stiff gliding, screaming. Is there nothing in my life that does not scream? Bees round the orange pom-poms of the buddleia. If I were ill it would explain so much. Perhaps my view of everything is distorted by illness, perhaps Parkside is a delusion. As an exercise in being-thankful-for-my-lot I try to think of neighbours I like, and I think immediately of 'the boys', of Wills with his slick hair and Charterhouse-and-army background and wicked

laugh, and Nikos with his wildly gay manners and wardrobe, and for a second I believe they are still here, and then I remember they are gone. The nicest people in the street, gone.

*Monday 20 May*
Tired. I am tired of myself.

Walked back from nursery with Linda. Harvey and Rhian rode their bikes on the pavement. Linda told me, as if she had just remembered it, that she had been a health visitor before Harvey, and to my great surprise I disbelieved her. All the way she asked me about Simon, where he practised, what his speciality was, how long we had been married. And then suddenly, as if she had had enough of me, she said, 'This way,' to Harvey, and turned off into Atwell Street. Superiority is a habit of hers. Perhaps it explains her appeal for me: what is complimentary is contradictory. I imagine making a confession to her, and her snubbing me. Is that what I want?

Headache again. Describe it. I can't.

Woken three times, twice by Tomos and once by Rhian.

*Tuesday 21 May*
Linda and Harvey's house for tea. We sat in their prim front room, Harvey and Rhian and Tomos playing in the back room. Linda was poised and talkative, describing her massage every Friday. 'I couldn't possibly relax if I didn't go.' Unexpectedly becoming intimate, girlish almost. 'Everything has

changed since Harvey. I mean *everything*.' Arching
her eyebrow. 'For a year we didn't have sex at all, not
once, and then it began again, and it was so different,
everything about it, because before he used to shout
"Yes, yes, yes", and now he shouts, "Wait, please
wait".' When she laughs she is especially beautiful.
Michael came in as she was laughing, and she started
to give me these looks and little smiles, as if we shared
a secret. 'We're very happy together,' she had said to
me, almost simpering. Why do I disbelieve her?

Chaos of bathtime. Simon singing to Tomos, non-
sense words to the tune of 'Here We Go Gathering
Nuts in May'; me reciting 'Jabberwocky'; Rhian –
pretending to be a seal – screaming, 'Gimme fish!
Gimme fish! Gimme fish!'; and Huw shouting, 'Shut
up, just shut up! I'm trying to *work*!' from next door
where he was playing with the computer. Exactly
Simon's tone, part despair, part rage. I need to be
emotionally numb, lobotomised. Or I lurch from one
mood to the next, from rage to tenderness in seconds,
and end up crying. Simon trying to be tender: 'What's
the matter with you, etc.'

Headache in the night. But I'm not ill. If I were
ill I wouldn't be able to take all this.

Woken three times by Tomos screaming. All the
usual tactics failed. His will-power is unbelievable.
My feelings extreme. Simon saying, 'We are not
bringing him up, we are engaged with him in a
death struggle.' I thought suddenly that I could
ask Linda about Tomos's sleep problems. She was
a health visitor, she would be able to give me

advice. But I would have to be sure Simon wouldn't find out.

It occurs to me: do I want to hear her advice about sleep problems or test whether or not she was a health visitor?

*Wednesday 22 May*
My tiredness. My lack of health. In the last year or two I have become sickly, susceptible to whatever virus or bug is going round. Simon says it is normal for me to be ill. I have normal amounts of illness for my time of life and circumstances. Simon and I constantly argue, we constantly fall back exhausted. I am desperate for a rest — a rest from myself, I don't want to be me anymore, it is unjust. Simon saying melodrama is the spirit of the age, 'savage farce we deserve', etc., how we all punish ourselves, lives of the martyrs. Me saying we have no extended family, we have no money, we have three children under seven. Simon exists on the theoretical level, and I on the practical, but it is the same thing.

Talking for the first time about separation, but it wouldn't work, it would only be harder for both of us.

*Thursday 23 May*
Hot. Horseflies on the river at 5 p.m. Simon home early for punting and picnic. Both of us, weary and seedy after three bad nights on the trot, surprised by tranquillity. The beauty of the river, the delight of the children at ducks, swans, overhanging greenery,

at the possibility of moorhens and water rats. Lying on my tummy on the warm wooden shelf at the end of the punt, looking into the water three inches below my nose, thinking, 'Just to slip into it, just to let it close over my head, what bliss.' Sunlight illuminated an incredible treasure of rubbish in the shallows: cans, bottles, crisp packets, cartons, all glowing in a green-golden nimbus. I thought if only my rubbishy life were lit like this.

Punted, to show that I could do it too, and at a critical moment the watch Daddy gave me for my eighteenth birthday fell off my wrist and disappeared into the water.

I resolved, finally, not to ask Linda's advice.

*Saturday 25 May*
Night of the Ainsling's dinner party.

When we arrived I realised I had been dreading it. Describe it. Michael dressed in paint-spattered corduroy trousers and T-shirt, Linda in red-and-black-flowered backless dress. Simon and I the only guests. Linda said, with a sparkle, 'A night off from the children' – as if she had five or six. One of my fainting auras came over me. For about an hour we settled the children upstairs in a variety of beds and cots.

Unexpectedly lovely dinner. Chilled cucumber soup, chicken casserole, profiteroles. Michael, apparently, is the cook. Nice wine. From the start Linda flirted with Simon, calling him 'doctor', asking him about his training, his work, etc., dipping her shoulders, presenting her cleavage. 'I've never been examined by a male doctor without feeling seduced.' Simon wittily attentive. Watching her, I felt almost excited, almost ready to acquiesce in whatever she might do, this dangerous beautiful woman.

As we began the casserole my headache returned. Michael and Simon were talking about writers who were doctors: Keats, Maugham, Chekhov, Bulgakov. Michael quoted Pritchett on Chekhov: 'The sad and farcical thing is that a man has an inner life'. The most interesting comment of the evening. I wanted to talk to him about Chekhov, but Linda kept asking me about the local schools, telling me about the shops in Bath, wondering out loud why the people in the street are so unfriendly.

By the time the profiteroles were finished I had fallen silent, thinking only of myself. Michael was drunk, Simon charming – as he is with other people. Thought again of how I wanted to write when I was young, how I was going to travel, live abroad, have affairs with foreign painters and film-makers and poets and be better than them, how I was going to be wanted, not wanting. And then I thought how tired I am of myself, tired even of my innocent girlish dreams of twenty years ago, how tired, and I began to pile up all my worries: the marriage, the money, Huw being bullied at school, Rhian's constant chatter, Tomos's crying at night; and as I piled them all up, I heard Tomos start to scream upstairs, and I got up automatically from the table without anyone even looking at me, and went up to him.

Sat for half an hour in the Ainsling's bedroom

feeding Tomos, looking at the mess. Expensive sexy dresses piled in front of one of the wardrobes. Downstairs the faint noises of conversation. After putting Tomos back I went to the bathroom and, coming out, there was Linda. 'I wanted to tell you how much I like your dress, I have a dress just like it.' She showed me dresses in their bedroom, oblivious of the mess: what do you think of this one, what about that one, the blue one would look good on you. Then something terrible happened. I started to talk. I couldn't help myself, I just started without knowing what I was doing, and I couldn't stop, I poured out everything, all the things I'd promised I would keep to myself. Standing there in her bedroom, with her dresses in my arms, talking and crying. A complete surrender to emotion. Talking about Tomos, the screaming, the sleeplessness, the refusal to eat, the headaches, the rows with Simon, the constant misery; it all came out, the hours up at night, the desperation, the boredom, the conviction that I was mentally ill. I talked for *twenty-five minutes*. I begged her to help me. I threw myself on her mercy.

Immediately afterwards overcome with shame. Linda sitting on the end of the bed, head down, playing with the hem of her red-and-black-flowered backless dress. For a minute or two we were both quiet. Then this: she said, 'I'm so glad we can tell each other things.' She said, 'I want to tell *you* something.' Confidential and purposeful, as if she had already forgotten everything I'd said. 'Next week,' she said, 'I'm going to have an abortion.'

There was a long pause, and her eyes never left mine. 'Oh,' I said. 'Michael and I were eight years trying for Harvey,' she said, 'and for the last two we've been trying to have another, we thought it was the only thing that would keep us together. But, you see, it's torn us apart. Now I'm pregnant, and next week I'm going to have an abortion.' She was still looking at me with those dreamy satisfied eyes. 'Why?' I murmured, dreading an answer. It seemed to be a question she hadn't expected. Turning away, she shrugged slightly. 'Complications,' she said quietly. 'There are complications.' I had a terror of this strange female suddenly. '*Medical* complications?' I asked in a whisper. 'Oh no,' she said, and sighed, scrutinising the open wardrobe as if seeing it for the first time. 'The problem is, it's not Michael's child.' We sat together on the bed for a minute in silence, it seemed like an hour, then we got up and went downstairs.

*Thursday 30 May*
In bed since Monday with what Simon calls 'run-of-the-mill tension migraine'. I have never had one before: I thought it was a stroke. A crushing, subtly shifting, always intensifying pain from the nape of my neck to my crown; the left side of my face numb; my vision blurred and the left side of my mouth stiff. Vomiting for thirty-six hours.

Straight after the Ainsling's party I began to feel unwell. On Sunday, in the evening, I left the house after a row with Simon and found myself by St

Thomas's. The door was unlocked; it was empty. I realised that in seven years living here I had never been inside. I sat in a pew trying to pray, and occasionally peeping round. A feeling of guilt and, perhaps, of fear. Fearful that by praying to a God I didn't believe in I would bring down His retribution. On the south wall of the chancel a picture of the 'hooly blisful martir', eyes heavenward, arms aloft; and that clumsy melodramatic picture made me think, despite myself, that there are always people – so many – in worse torment than me. Don't know how long I sat there. In the end formulated the requests: please let me be a better wife, please let me be a better mother, please let me *survive*. The church is late Victorian, big and plain inside, kept very neat by local women. Irises on either side of the altar. After a while I came out and thought to myself: so I have overcome my anger. Only then I realised that I had prayed for no one but myself. That night the migraine began.

My life has changed and will never be the same again.

*Friday 31 May*
5 p.m., pushing Tomos through the park. Describe it. Dancing pinpricks of light off ripples in the big lake. Boy wearing football shorts wading across small pond for benefit of his friends, all giggling. Loud birdsong. Cypresses casting thick shadows on the bright grass. Smell of warmth: warm grass, warm park benches. The arrival of summer, or something like that.

# BETH WYT TI MOEN?

## I

It was the middle of June 1993, and the Harrises were
deep in West Wales with their two children. Like
needles in a haystack, Dr Harris thought. They were
staying with his wife's aunt and uncle in their converted farmhouse, a crooked slate-grey shape buried
like abandoned machinery in a deserted wooded valley twenty miles south-east of Cardigan. The name
of the house was 'Gweledigaeth'. Dr Harris's three-
and-a-half-year-old son Huw had seen two buzzards,
a jay, a barn owl, and something 'huge, with a face like
a Lappet-faced vulture or something like that' floating
over their steep, narrow valley. His son was obsessed
with birds.

The freshness of May had been replaced by dull,
melancholy heat liable at any time to give way to
rain.

It was late afternoon, and it had been a hard day.
In the morning, as soon as they arrived at the beach,
it began to pour, and when they got home Ffion
discovered she had left her handbag in the car park.
Huw had been sick, twice on the first journey to the
beach and once more on the second. 'He's taking

liberties,' Dr Harris said. 'He knows his father's a doctor.' Huw's neck and chest were covered in a pink rash resembling a scald, and he was running a temperature of 103. 'Rubella,' Dr Harris said. 'You can't get less ill.' Huw threw up his lunch and was put to bed with his bird books, blanket and parrot glove puppet. Later Ffion also went to bed, with a headache, leaving Dr Harris with Rhian, the six-month-old baby.

For the last quarter of an hour he had been trying to change her. She was writhing on Aunt Myfanwy's bed and he was contorted over her, straining like a man attempting to thread a needle by brute force. 'No!' he shouted. 'Rhian, no!' She screamed and plunged as if he were applying hot metal to her.

As he struggled he hypothesised a medical condition called Baby Rage. It afflicts parents, he thought. Aunt Myfanwy's bedroom, with its claustrophobic pastel shades, lace trims, flower theme and low ceiling (against which he had knocked his head three times), mocked him, and he felt Baby Rage building steadily in him.

'Don't you dare!' he shouted at his daughter. Her tear-filled eyes fixed him with a look of violent accusation he could not meet.

For ten minutes they struggled together as equals, the outcome uncertain, and then her nappy snapped open. Off-balance, Dr Harris put his hand into the tub of zinc and caster oil cream, swore, knocked the mug of warm water off the bedstead and trod in the bin liner full of soiled nappies.

Raising a fist to the room, he discovered the nappy attached to it by one of its adhesive tabs, and swung his arm violently to shake it off. It left his hand at an angle of thirty degrees to the horizontal and went through the open casement window into the front garden below.

'What are you doing to her?' Ffion was shouting through the door which he kept shut with his heels. In the background he thought he heard Huw crying.

'Doing to her?' Dr Harris yelled back. 'I'm not doing anything to her, how do you expect me to do anything to her?'

Downstairs, in the hallway of the converted farmhouse, Ffion's uncle was greeting their guests – his Welsh niece Eluned, her Yorkshire husband Nick, and their two children – whose collective first impression was of bloody violence being perpetrated somewhere in the upper reaches of the house.

'Go into the sitting room,' Uncle Gwilym said. 'Tea's ready.' Aunt Myfanwy came out of the kitchen to greet them, her voice obscured by the sounds of atrocity from above. Something fell past the sitting-room window which they all saw. With half-smiles they sat down, and Uncle Gwilym engaged Nick in conversation about the main motorway routes of the country.

'Tell me,' he said. 'Do you get much use out of the M4?'

'Open the door!' Ffion was shouting for all to hear.

But Dr Harris did not hear, the sounds of his daughter's and his own anguish deafened him, carrying not only downstairs but out into the garden and surrounding fields, alarming pigeons and blackbirds which racketed out of nearby trees.

Ffion forced an entrance.

'Give her to me,' she said. Her daughter, an extraordinary crimson, reached towards her.

'I'm comforting her!' Dr Harris shouted, moving away. 'Can't you *see* I'm comforting her!'

They danced together between bed and wardrobe, knocking over the bin, a chair and the linen basket, their heavy footsteps sounding downstairs like drunken uproar, and eventually the screaming infant passed from one parent to the other. Empty-handed, Dr Harris stood in the doorway panting, pressing his thumbs into his eyes. Ffion stood by the opposite wall, rocking her daughter who clung to her, her crumpled face battened onto her shoulder. There was no peace from her screaming.

'Paid becso, Rhian bach, ma' mami yma,' Ffion murmured.

From time to time, in between Rhian's screams, Huw could be heard yelling down the corridor.

'What have you done to her?' Ffion said quietly when she could. 'Why is your face covered in cream?' Her shoulders trembled with the force of her self-control. Dr Harris stood rigidly in the doorway.

'I've done nothing,' he replied. He used a bitter, violent voice. There was a smart dash of cream across his forehead and two blots on his eyebrows. 'What have I done? Nothing, I've done nothing, less than nothing. Look at her. I've spent the last half hour trying to dress her. Is she dressed? Not even you could claim she's dressed, she's naked, she's not wearing anything at all. She was wearing more when I started.' His voice rose half an octave. 'I haven't *done* anything, she won't *let* me do anything, she refuses to be dressed, she insists on being undressed, she insists on lashing out at me, she insists on kicking off her clothes and *wallowing in her waste fluids*. I'll tell you one thing.' He paused. 'She's got your temper.' He stood, fists clenched, by the door, wondering, despite himself, whether he had gone too far. 'I did try,' he added. 'I promise you I tried.'

'I don't know what you're talking about, Simon. I can't understand a thing you say.'

'I'm talking about anguish. What else is there to talk about?'

'I thought with the second you wouldn't be like this.'

'I am like this. *She's* like this.'

Ffion crooned in Welsh to her daughter. She had stopped crying and was looking at Dr Harris over her mother's shoulder, the most beautiful baby he had ever seen, her nipple-sucking-shaped mouth a perfect pink, her eyes as round and blue as a cartoon bird's.

'You think it's worse because she's a girl, don't you?' Dr Harris said, looking away. 'Don't you?'

'Paid becso, paid becso, ma' mami yma,' Ffion said softly to her daughter.

'What are you saying to her?' Dr Harris demanded.

'I can't follow. Tell me what you're saying to the little sod.'

'Calm down. Go and see to Huw.'

'Don't provoke me. I want to know what you've just said.'

'I'm comforting her.'

'I've already done that. She's had plenty of bloody comforting.'

Dr Harris stood silently in the doorway, outraged. Already he was outraged by his own behaviour. His beautiful daughter was looking at him with her big wet eyes.

Ffion said, 'Bydd mami'n aros nes bod ti'n well. Will you never learn? Go on, see to Huw.'

He turned, exited smartly, and there was a crack as his head hit the door frame.

'What do the kids want to drink? Squash?' Aunt Myfanwy poured tea into Nick's cup which he held in his large outstretched palm as if it were loose change to be counted. They sat in the living room among the antiques under the white-washed ceiling with its dark low-hanging beams. The walls were white-washed too, and stippled to create a rustic effect; you only had to brush against them to bleed. The shouting upstairs had died to a murmur which, in the gaps in the conversation, they all strained to make out. Aunt Myfanwy sat on the Louis Quatorze, Nick and Eluned on the Chippendale. Their children – Harry, aged thirteen, and Alicia-Marie, aged ten – lolled on floor cushions, models of preoccupation.

Through the leaded lights of the windows they saw Cardiganshire fields, sky and clouds the colour of slate in the afternoon light, swart oaks, humped fruit trees. Uncle Gwilym came in solemnly with a plate of Welsh cakes.

'Have you got juice?' Nick asked. He spoke loudly with a Yorkshire accent. 'I don't hold with squash, not with all these chemicals you get in it. Different from when I were a kid. If you haven't got juice, give them water, they drink water at home, they know what's good for them.'

As Aunt Myfanwy went into the kitchen, Ffion appeared carrying Rhian who was dressed in a plaid dress and red cotton socks. Everyone coo'ed. She was the most beautiful baby they had ever seen, they said. Her cheeks were purple and yellow. 'A little temper tantrum,' Ffion said. To Rhian she murmured, 'Paid bod yn swil, cariad, mae pawb wedi dod i weld ti.'

Sunlight fell at her feet in loose squares like bright clothing shed onto the floor, and her daughter pressed her face into her neck. As she sat down on the sofa they slowly resumed their conversation.

Dr Harris could not hear the murmur downstairs as he walked along the corridor to his son's room where Huw was chanting an obscure phrase. He opened the door and went in, and the chanting abruptly stopped. From his position at the wrong end of the bed Huw silently examined his father. He was sitting cross-legged with the duvet bunched around him like a tepee and the contents of Ffion's make-up bag scattered in his lap.

'What is it, Huw?' Dr Harris said. He used his soft voice.

'You're not *cross*,' Huw said, staring.

'No, I'm not cross.'

'You're just *tired*.'

'That's right. What's the matter? Can't you sleep? Do you still feel hot?'

'Why have you got all that on your face?'

Dr Harris ignored this. 'What's the matter, Huw?'

'But why?'

'Never mind.' Dr Harris wiped his face with his shirt sleeve. 'What's the matter, do you feel sick again?'

Huw threw lipsticks and eyeliner pencils into the air, and chanted, 'Need a wee! Need a wee! Need a wee!'

Dr Harris went to straighten the duvet.

'What's happened here, Huw?' he said.

Huw scrambled away, saying nothing.

'What's this?'

'The bed is full of wee,' Huw said.

'Did you have a little accident?' He used his soft, sympathetic voice.

'Well,' Huw said. 'More wee than an accident came out.'

'Did it?'

'It did. From my wee-er.'

'Did it happen when you were asleep?'

'Well.' Huw thought about this. 'I was kept awake.'

'What do you mean, kept awake?'

'I was kept awake by the noise.'

'What noise?'

'The noise of the weeing.'

They went hand in hand to the bathroom (Dr Harris knocking his head against the door once and scraping his elbows on the walls twice) where they resumed their conversation, Huw sitting low on the toilet and Dr Harris perched on the edge of the bath.

'Have you finished?'

'I haven't.'

'Hurry up, there's a good boy.'

'What's that noise?'

'What noise now?'

'That noise then. Like a woodpecker or something. A woodpecker or something like that.'

'Perhaps it is a woodpecker. There are probably woodpeckers in the woods.'

'Why?'

'I'm not saying there are, there might be.'

'Why aren't they?'

'There might be, there might not be, I'm not committing myself.'

'What woodpeckers? Where are the woodpeckers?'

'Huw, I don't know. Have you finished? Don't sit like that on the toilet, you'll fall in.'

'What will you say?'

'What do you mean, what will I say?'

'What will you say if I go doobydoobydoobydooby?' He waggled his head, and Dr Harris frowned. 'Into the toilet,' Huw explained.

'I'll be very sad,' Dr Harris said. 'Come on now. You must have finished.'

'I haven't finished.'

'Come on please Huw, hurry up.'

'What woodpeckers, Daddy?'

'When we get you back into bed I'll read to you about woodpeckers from your book. How about that?'

'Daddy?'

'Yes?'

'Do you know, Great Spotty Woodpeckers are quite small.'

'I'm sure they are. We'll read all about Great Spotty Woodpeckers. Please hurry up.'

'They've got a *sticky tongue*.'

'Have they?'

'For eating insects. Like *giant wood wasps*.'

'Wipe now. Come on, give yourself a wipe. Use this.'

'Green Woodpeckers are hugely big.'

'I'm sure you're right. No, a wipe, a *wipe*.'

'Big as that.' Huw spread his arms out and slipped into the toilet with a yell.

In the sitting room there was a slight pause in the conversation which continued, out of respect to Ffion, almost immediately. Nick was talking, and Eluned was holding and admiring Rhian. Nick wanted to know where the Harrises lived, what sort of house they lived in, how long they had been living there.

Ffion said, 'I think it must be three years. Or

four. I can't remember. That's the sort of place it is, it's the sort of place where you lose track of time. Very restful.'

Nick said, 'You're probably looking at a reduction in value of between ten and twenty per cent over the last three years. Am I right?'

'I've no idea,' Ffion said.

'He was a property dealer,' Eluned said. 'Until the market collapsed.' Her voice was very soft and her hair was a very pale blonde cut short. It was obvious that she adored her husband.

His son and daughter watched him as he talked. They adored him too. Harry had a thin face and brown hair cut in a fashionable style. Alicia-Marie, who sat next to him on the floor cushions with her knees hugged to her chest, kept asking, 'Why, Dad?' Her dad was the centre of attention.

He was in his mid-forties, a powerful, heavy man, like an athlete gone to seed. His polo shirt was tight over his belly, his tennis shorts cut into his pale thighs. His face was fleshy and strained, and bulged when he talked. He talked ceaselessly. Sitting heavily in his chair, occasionally flexing his arms, as if to draw attention to the old tattoos on his biceps (greying designs of obscure perhaps mythological subjects, vulgar figurations symbolising love and death), he talked in a loud self-confident voice.

'Had them done when I were in the paras,' he said. 'I were that daft. I look at them now, and I say to myself, "You live with your mistakes." That's what I tell these lot.' He gestured at Harry and Alicia-Maria.

'Don't make mistakes. You'll never get shot of them. Not that they listen to me. The boy don't.' Harry blushed. 'What am I forever telling you?' his father asked. 'Eh?'

There was a silence as Dr Harris came into the room. The baby-beater. Sensing the awkwardness of the moment, he stroked his daughter's head, and circled the table towards the window seat.

'Your wife's been telling us how your lad's sick,' Nick said. His opinion of Dr Harris showed in the pugnacious tilt of his face and his flat, disbelieving look.

Dr Harris made a mild gesture of unconcern totally at odds with the impression he had already made. 'Nothing serious. Rubella. Usual symptoms, mild fever, slight inflammation of the lymph nodes. Some vomiting. Not serious. Infectious, however. Wouldn't do to bring him down.' He used his offhand casual voice.

Nick grunted. 'Handy having a quack in the family.'

In the window behind Dr Harris the afternoon light was deepening, the sky a muffled pattern of packed cloud, mottled shell-pink and summer-shadow blue at the horizon. Wishing that he were out enjoying the last warmth of the day instead of sitting inside with his wife's aunt's guests, Dr Harris examined Nick who had begun to talk again, and sensed at once that he would go on and on. He immediately began to chew his lower lip. It had been a hard day, and he did not think he could stand further provocation.

'Tea, Simon?' Aunt Myfanwy asked. 'Gwilym, put the kettle on. Nick,' she added, 'tell us again where you're working now.'

For the last hour Nick had been talking about himself, about his upbringing, his various careers, his efforts to bring up his children. His commitment to his family was simple and consuming; he was an indefatigable father who adhered to a credo of hard work and self-belief, and was not afraid to be censorious. 'The boy's that daft,' he said severely. 'I never stop telling you, do I, eh?' His own life had been irregular: after colourful careers in the forces, industry and various types of business, he had become a management consultant, working out of a single room in an ex-parish hall in Sheffield. Business was poor; he worked the telephone for twelve hours a day, then went home and studied for his exams until midnight. 'I tell these lot,' he said, nodding towards his children, 'not to make the mistakes I made.' His vigour and faith seemed solid physical properties, like his thick face or tattooed arms, and Dr Harris disliked him intensely, feeling him somehow responsible for the misery of his day.

The children, especially Harry, were mesmerised by him. Slowly, as Nick talked, another hour passed.

Dr Harris drank three cups of tea and chewed his thumbnail until it bled.

Gradually the light through the window behind him turned orange. Uncle Gwilym looked at his watch and went to open a bottle of wine.

\*   \*   \*

From time to time Dr Harris tried to catch Ffion's eye, and once he stood to offer to take Rhian, but Ffion looked the other way, and he took some sandwiches instead. After a while he began to suffer from stomach cramps which he also associated with Nick. Shifting from side to side in his seat to alleviate the pain, he imagined telling Nick to shut up. The satisfaction he derived from this was minimal. Every ten minutes he looked at his watch and each time he was horrified to see how long he had spent listening to Nick. He told himself that he had never heard such self-regarding rubbish. *It's the children I feel for*, he thought. Through the windows shadows were slowly lengthening over the lawn as if dragging down the apple trees and brambles.

'Every Saturday morning I take them to the gym,' Nick was saying. 'Keep fit. Alicia-Marie loves it, don't you pet; the boy's got lazy, he'd rather stay in bed. But we don't underestimate fitness in our family. I've told them. They know how serious it is.'

He sat before them, overweight, florid and pugnacious. Dr Harris fidgeted.

'When you've been in the paras like me,' Nick went on, 'you don't lose your fitness, you know how to keep it. It's basic. I work out every week. I can do a hundred press-ups without breaking sweat. I'm as fit now as I was when I was seventeen.'

'Surely not,' Dr Harris said before he could stop himself. It was the first thing he had said for an hour and a half, and with the singleness of a tennis crowd everyone in the room turned to him.

There was a pause.

'How's that?' Nick said.

'Just a medical point,' Dr Harris said. 'Nothing personal.' He felt himself blush.

'What point?'

'Well,' Dr Harris said, 'speaking medically, a man of, say, forty-five is simply not capable of the same level of physical performance as he was at, say, seventeen; muscles and organs degenerate over time, the efficiency of the lungs and heart diminishes, pupillary and other reflexes malfunction, and so on. What I mean is, it's not simply a question of fitness.' Even as he spoke he wondered how awful he sounded. He did not dare look at Ffion.

'I'll show you,' Nick said, to Dr Harris's alarm, and suddenly got up.

There was a slight pause in which they all wondered what this might mean, and Aunt Myfanwy cleared her throat as if to say something.

'No, no,' Dr Harris said. 'You miss my point.'

'I'll do a hundred press-ups for you now. It's no bother.'

'It's not necessary,' Dr Harris said, attempting to smile. 'Really.'

'No bother at all.'

Dr Harris continued to smile, out of pure embarrassment. 'I hope you aren't interpreting what I said as some sort of challenge,' he said.

'No challenge in it far as I can see. All you got to do is count to a hundred. I reckon you can do that.'

Harry and Alice-Maria laughed, and Dr Harris,

feeling the situation well beyond him, slowly got to his feet.

'Don't be ridiculous,' Ffion said.

Nick was swinging his fat arms, his belly shifting up and down. 'That's it,' he said encouragingly.

'At least you'll have a doctor on hand if you do have a heart attack,' Dr Harris said. He wished he hadn't said this.

Eluned looked at her husband with almost flirtatious pride. 'Well,' she said. 'Don't think we're all going to troop out and watch.'

'Can *we* watch?' Harry asked, jumping up. 'Can we Dad, can we?'

'You?' his father said in disgust. 'You stay here and look after your mother like I taught you.' He looked over to Dr Harris. 'Ready?' Tucking his polo shirt tightly into his shorts, he went out of the room into the vestibule, and Dr Harris followed him.

## II

Outside the air was grey. The sunset was elsewhere, and the last weak light was bleaching the colours out of the grey-green trees and brown-and-grey outhouse walls. Elongated shadows striped the ground. The featureless sky was smooth and dim. It was a time for reflection and contemplation, not action. The two men took their bearings and moved off.

Nick went first, and Dr Harris followed. He could not keep his eyes off the thick bulk of Nick's shoulders, the slight movement of the flesh of his neck, he watched it with a sort of sensual attraction. They went diagonally across the limestone-chip driveway and round the side of the barn where Uncle Gwilym kept his car, to a plot of cropped grass between the barn wall and the edge of the trees which fell steeply to the valley bottom. Raspberry bushes ran along the barn side, and a mildewed caravan stood under a large elm.

'This'll do,' Nick said.

Dr Harris looked round and sniffed. There was a sour smell of earth. From somewhere deeper in the valley came birdsong and the sound of water, elements of a peace no less deep for being banal. The sudden move out of the darkened house into the light and spaciousness of the countryside disoriented him, and his thoughts were confused.

Nick was saying something.

'Sorry?' he said.

'I said, better count out loud so as you know I'm not cheating.' Nick was sitting on his knees on the grass, with his belly hanging over his waistband, looking up at him, and Dr Harris stared down as if seeing him for the first time, transfixed by the man's physicality, his pale wide arms and broad face, already mottled, and thighs bursting from his tight shorts. He felt juvenile suddenly, he was reminded of his schooldays, summer afternoons sprawling on playing fields, arguing and watching other boys fight. It occurred to him that Nick might actually have a heart attack. 'Wait a minute,' he said, trying to regain some composure.

'It doesn't really interest me how many press-ups you can do. What I mean is, I'll take your word for it. It's not as if we're obliged to go back and announce some sort of score.' He would have said more, but before he had chance Nick had begun.

'Count then,' Nick said with a grunt, after a moment.

'Sorry,' Dr Harris said. He began to count. 'Five, six, seven . . .'

From time to time Nick let out a fierce hiss of breath. His body shook as he pushed himself up and down, and Dr Harris stared at it with fascination, he could not remember seeing anything so powerful and ugly.

'Thirteen, fourteen,' he counted. He used an efficient voice which was occasionally betrayed by a stammer. Once or twice he looked nervously over his shoulder to see if anyone had followed them out of the house.

'Twenty, twenty-one . . .'

'Missed out nineteen,' Nick said between two great hisses, astonishing Dr Harris. It astonished him that Nick could still speak.

'Sorry,' he said again.

Soon it was obvious that Nick was going to succeed. Dr Harris was too amazed to be embarrassed any more. As he counted he stared at Nick's great white arms, and in only five or six minutes Nick was completing the last few push-ups. He passed the hundred mark without acknowledgement, and kept going.

'Well done,' Dr Harris said. Nick said nothing. Regularly, every five or six seconds, he let out a loud hiss of breath.

At a hundred and twenty-three Dr Harris moved off a little way and stood by the caravan.

At a hundred and forty he stopped counting.

'Yes,' he said shortly. 'Well done.'

Nick said nothing, he hissed and wheezed and kept going. In a little while he began to perform one-arm press-ups, first on his right arm, then on his left. After a few minutes he reverted to two-arm press-ups, introduced a clap at the end of each upstroke, then went back to one-arm press-ups. His physical inexhaustibility was as dreadful as the monotony of his conversation.

'Impressive,' Dr Harris said, and when he received no answer to this he turned and walked out of the grassy plot back towards the house.

Immediately there was a shout, and Nick came after him. He caught up with him where the drive turned to grass and they stood facing each other.

'Yes?' Dr Harris said. He didn't feel like talking. He wanted to go inside and forget what had happened. Now it seemed the man was going to try to humiliate him.

Nick was gulping air, his face red and wet, attempting to speak.

'Wait a moment,' Dr Harris said. 'Get your breath back.'

'You're a doctor,' Nick began, and stopped. There was a pause.

'I am,' Dr Harris said, struck by the oddity of this gambit.

They stood there in the dim light, not saying anything, listening to far-off birdsong and the occasional lament of sheep in the field behind the house. A solitary crow passed silently overhead.

'I just need a word,' Nick said at last. 'Advice.' He wiped his forehead with a hand, glanced over to the house and back again. He seemed to need prompting.

'You mean *medical* advice?'

There was a longer pause as Nick gathered himself together.

'It's the sex,' he said finally.

'I see,' Dr Harris said. He used a neutral voice. 'What exactly about the sex?'

Nick looked all round, at the house, the driveway, the trees, the sky, the caravan, the raspberry bushes, and when there was no part of the scene left to look at, at Dr Harris.

'I can't keep it up as long as I used to.'

'I see.'

'I know there's drugs,' he said quickly. Dr Harris nodded and Nick fell silent again.

'Drugs are only useful in some cases in fact,' Dr Harris said. 'Impotence can be organic, that is to say caused by a physical condition; or psychogenic, which is to say, mental or emotional. Without knowing your history, I can't really offer any advice. You would have to see your GP.'

Nick said nothing.

'Of course, it's perfectly possible,' Dr Harris continued, gradually settling to routine phrases, 'that impotence isn't the problem at all, it depends what you mean by it. When you say impotence, what do you mean, do you mean a lack of sexual desire, or the inability to penetrate, or failure to ejaculate, or what?'

'I can't manage more than two hours,' Nick said. 'Two, two and a half at most.'

Dr Harris stared at him. 'I'm sorry?' he said.

'I used to be able to keep going all night. Four, five hours. Not any more. There's something wrong with me, I need the right drugs.'

There was a pause while Dr Harris took this in.

'I'm afraid I don't understand. Did you say four or five hours?'

'Used to come two, three times, and now it's once and I've nothing left.' He was becoming emotional, working his jaw and rubbing his face with his hand.

'Just a minute. You used to have sex for *four hours*, and now you can't last for more than two?' Dr Harris was becoming annoyed. But to his amazement Nick began to cry.

'For Christ's sake,' he said sobbing. 'You've got to help me, there must be drugs for it, it doesn't matter what they are, I'll take them, I can't bear it, I can't talk to the wife about it, I'm living a lie, it's like some bloody awful secret, some bloody awful bloody secret. Please,' he said. 'Please, you've got to help me. Please.' He spoke the last words into his hands.

'Oh,' Dr Harris said, not knowing what to say.

He could not take his eyes off the top of Nick's head.

'What I mean is,' Dr Harris said. 'What I mean,' he said, 'is that, well, two hours is an unusually *long* time for which to perform intercourse.'

Nick looked up, his face wet. 'Not for me it isn't,' he said aggressively.

Dr Harris made a vague noise without meaning.

'What'll the wife think?' Nick demanded. 'Bloody hell! There are drugs can help me, I know there are. Hormones is what I want.'

'Hormones?' Dr Harris said. '*Hormones*? Are you joking? You'd explode. You must be stuffed with hormones.'

Nick worked his jaw and looked away down the driveway. There was another long silence, and Dr Harris recovered to the extent that he nearly laughed out loud. He didn't think he had ever heard anything so ridiculous. His face twitched as he tried to keep his self-control.

'It's the bloody end,' Nick said simply.

This was hilarious. But Dr Harris suddenly shut his mouth and took a step back, appalled. Between his lungs he felt a sharp pain and the hot dizziness associated with the onset of primary pulmonary hypertension. His vision failed, he seemed to see a moving darkness in front of him, and without warning he suffered the insight that he was and always would be a failure. This conviction came to him unexpectedly, out of nowhere, and obliterated all thoughts of Nick. Horrified, he saw himself failing through the rest of his life, failing constantly and inevitably and without anyone at all to blame except himself, failing as much as it is humanly possible to fail; he saw that there would be no difficulties to which he did not succumb, no decisions he would not get wrong, no arguments he would avoid escalating, no opportunities of love he did not squander; he saw himself bringing nothing but disappointment and misery to everyone he knew; he would be a joyless, burdensome husband, an aggrieved and didactic parent and a GP with no prospects for ever – and the shock of this insight was so great he staggered sideways and put his hand out as if he would fall onto the limestone-chip driveway. In the same instant he thought of Ffion, Huw and Rhian with a longing so desperate it was almost savage, he groaned out loud, his vision cleared, and he suddenly found himself standing as before in front of Nick.

'What's that?' Nick said, looking at him sharply, and Dr Harris stood there, his legs trembling, looking back, not knowing what to say, hardly knowing what he was doing there.

Almost a minute passed.

'Intercourse lasts, on average, ten minutes for me,' he said, attempting a smile.

Nick's face showed his horror. 'I don't know why you're telling me that,' he said in disgust. 'You're a bloody doctor.' He looked as if he would spit.

'Well,' Dr Harris said. 'We were talking about intercourse.'

'I'm talking about my *marriage*,' Nick said loudly,

and pushing past Dr Harris, he went quickly across the edge of the grey drive towards the house.

## III

Late that night, long after everyone had gone to bed, Dr Harris lay awake. There was a skylight in the high ceiling of the room through which he watched the faint movements of black clouds across the black sky.

Ffion woke and without moving said, 'What is it?'

'Doesn't matter.'

For several minutes there was silence and he thought she had fallen asleep again.

'What?' she asked.

There was another long silence, and then he sighed, and said in a whisper, 'I'm sorry.'

He waited for her to say something, but in the quiet he heard the sound of her breathing grow regular and deep. He leaned over and looked at her sleeping face, and then he got up and went over to Rhian's cot.

She was lying across it diagonally, astride the quilt, snoring, her small, blunt features tilted upwards and her hair splayed above her head. Her skin was amazingly pale. For a while Dr Harris stood watching her sleep, then he lifted her out of her cot and carried her slowly downstairs and outside into the bland moonlit darkness.

He stood on the edge of the driveway where he had stood with Nick, with his daughter in his arms, and after a minute she woke. She looked at her father with sleepy eyes, and slowly lifted a hand to his face.

Dr Harris stroked her head. 'Dadi gwlyb,' he said with the slow and formal emphasis of a Welsh learner. Rhian began to cry.

'Ust Rhian love,' he whispered. 'Don't cry. Daddy's yma.'

The trees over the driveway were black against the mauve sky, and the stars were clear and white overhead. 'Paid cry, Rhian,' Dr Harris whispered, bending his face over hers. 'Daddy's here. Beth wyt ti the matter, Rhian?' He could not remember any more Welsh, and his efforts to speak it broke down. Crying gently, his daughter seemed to be looking past him up into the sky, and he looked up too.

'Look, Rhian,' he said. 'The stars. The Plough. And Orion the Hunter. And the Great Bear.'

Rhian seemed to look, and without a thought in his head he began to whisper to her the stories he half-remembered of the constellations – Orion who boasted he could kill anything and was fatally stung by a snake or scorpion; the beautiful Andromeda abandoned for some reason to a sea-monster; Hercules destroyed by his wife on account of some appalling mistake that Dr Harris could not bring to mind, all transformed in death. Somewhere in the woods an owl hooted, and his dry voice went on and on.

# MASTURBATORY

July 1996. Michael is in the bathroom masturbating.
The bathroom is tiny, a recess stolen from the third
bedroom when, at some point during the seventies,
a previous occupant moved the bathroom upstairs.
It is so small it has a sliding door. The angle of the
roof makes a shower possible only on bended knees.
The joke is that the room is exactly the size of two
baths, half of which is taken up with the bath, half
by the toilet, and half by the washbasin. But this
does not take into account the cupboard, cistern
or radiator. Or for that matter the person using the
bathroom. For some reason the fittings are the largest
commercially available: king-size, triple-tiered pine
towel-rail, baroque hand-carved toilet-roll holder,
cabinet-shaped toilet-brush holder. The bathroom
is the creation of a wit or retard.

Michael uses his thumb and index finger in short
bursts, drifting off into reverie. His penis shows a
marked bias to the left, and has a twitching life of its
own; its skin is grey, a crooked blue vein dogging the
upperside not vivid like a blue vein in stilton but dull
like ink in a biro. It is Friday, mid-morning. Parkside
is hushed, feminine. Parkside is defined by women
and their babies, Michael thinks; he has learnt this in

the months of his unemployment, walking the streets in the quiet late morning or early afternoon, feeling himself fall into a slower, more purposeful rhythm. At those times, it seems to him, women give Parkside its identity, deepening its tone, clarifying its details, affecting somehow even its architecture, the orderly bay windows, the fancy gables, the pretty ornamental brickwork.

As he thinks this, Michael continues to masturbate. He is naked except for some articles of his wife's clothing: black stockings, a black lace suspender belt decorated with red roses and a matching brassière. The brassière cuts uncomfortably into his armpits. It's funny, he thinks, what habits you get into when you've too much time on your hands. He tries to recall a corresponding scene from his reading, but can't.

Frustratingly, his reveries are often unerotic, even anti-erotic. Although he tries to concentrate on the diminutive Korean go-go dancer he once saw in New York, or the large-breasted middle-aged woman with too-elegant hair who used to live over the road, he soon ends up thinking of himself masturbating in a ridiculous bathroom, of the futility, perhaps even the insubstantiality of his desires. He can't concentrate – the result of his long unemployment. His thought processes are masturbatory. Masturbation he defines as the inability to concentrate on the real world. As he masturbates, he chews his free thumb nail or gazes vacantly at the richly pine-clad toilet cistern.

★   ★   ★

As soon as she arrives at Mr Polunin's house Janine starts the laundry, washes the kitchen floor, cleans the fridge and empties the bins. Every few minutes she uses her inhaler. Then it is time to go into the conservatory and sit with a coffee and the local newspaper in one of the narrow wicker chairs. It is bright under the glass roof, sunlight stamps the flagged floor and scatters across the spider plants, the cacti, the potted miniature orange trees, the musk orchids. They are beautiful, but today she is disapproving. She can't explain but she doesn't feel right. It is a feeling she has never had before: as if she's not at the centre of her life, but at the edge of it. Last night she argued with her mother about her membership of the League of Young Evangelists which she would like to let lapse, then her sister came home with a boy and smoked five cigarettes in the living room. She reads her paper, winding a strand of hair around a finger.

Local police have launched a knife amnesty after a spate of city attacks. Fire ripped through a barn in Cholmonley Bottom, destroying twenty-five bales of hay. A tombola held at St Thomas's garden fête raised over £500 for Age Concern. She flicks through impatiently until she reaches a report on page thirteen headed *Lake of Evil*. At the County Court on Monday's session, a man and woman were charged with the attempted murder of the woman's husband. The character of the crime was unusual, the culmination of a short, sordid sequence of events. The husband was the owner of a medium-sized manufacturer of garden appliances, and moderately wealthy. It was imperative to the would-be murderers that his death should appear accidental in order that his widow could claim the insurance. The plan they devised was this. After dinner one evening the woman would arouse her husband and induce him to make love to her on the floor of their dining room. The French windows leading to their large garden would be conveniently open. While they were engaged in love-making, her lover would creep in, overpower the husband, and together with the wife suffocate him with a cushion. From the living room they would carry the already-undressed corpse through the garden and deposit it in the small weed-filled lake where he was known to swim every morning and where he would be found floating face down the following day. This plan was the plan of a wit or retard. It began well. The husband was making love to his wife on the dining-room floor when the woman's lover assaulted him with the pillow. But the husband fended him off and escaped through the French windows into the garden. Finding his motorised lawnmower (a product of his own firm) parked against the patio, he drove off at high speed across the lawn, his naked wife and her lover pursuing him closely. The mower was defective, he lost control of it, and it plunged into the lake, knocking him senseless. But, as his wife and her lover ran up, he recovered and swam across the lake to the other side, where he pulled himself out and sprinted wet and naked into the village to raise the alarm. In his summing up the judge commended him for his great spirit and presence of mind.

It disgusts her. She is disgusted with herself. She screws up the paper and carries it into the kitchen where she throws it into her bag with her copy of the St Thomas Church magazine and two dozen leaflets to be posted for the League of Young Evangelists.

'No man would look at you twice,' her sister had said.

The dining-room floor, she thinks. Or the flagged floor of a conservatory.

It is hot in the tiny bathroom. On the rounded top of a towel over the triple-decker rail he has laid out, in advance, two wads of toilet tissue, one for the first rush, the other for drips.

Bored, and wanting to conclude the episode as soon as possible so he can get back to the book he has left lying open in the bedroom, he concentrates on an image of his wife leaning forward over the kitchen table, her hair falling across her face, her cardiganed breasts coming to rest on the surface, a mundane image but one he uses, like a worn picture torn from a magazine, when all else fails. It is immediately effective. He makes a grab for the first wad of tissue, drops it on the floor and, as he bends for it, his back seizes.

The pain is intense, lifting him onto his tiptoes. The only noise he is able to make is a long, high-pitched grunt located deep in his body, sounding oddly ecstatic. Even in the midst of his pain he can't help noticing, with a sense of shame and awe, that his erection continues.

After a while he realises that something serious has happened. He cannot move. He is bent over with his hands dangling between his knees, his forehead resting on the lip of the washbasin and his feet straddling the dropped tissue which is his main view. One stocking has slipped down; the suspender belt cuts into his belly. He feels himself locked into a controtionist's finale, and his erection mocks him, waving gently.

After a while longer he has another insight: he is permanently stuck. All movement is impossible. He considers this. He is fixed like an exhibit in the tiny bathroom, wearing his wife's badly-fitting underwear, frozen in an act of ostentatious self-abuse, in need of medical assistance.

A few more minutes pass, and he begins to utter the long, high-pitched grunt again. He has remembered that his wife and three-year-old son are due home soon. His wife had mentioned to him that her parents might be coming for lunch. The noise he makes goes on and on.

Nothing disgusts her more than stories of sex offenders, intruders and peeping Toms: they are one of her guilty pleasures. She believes in the struggle of good and evil, and knows it to be true in her own life. All the time she is dusting the living room, she is thinking of the bedroom, and what Mr Polunin might have left in it this time.

Soon there is a smell of polish through the whole house. The ironing is done, the last of the washing is hanging on the line, the rooms are as clean and carefully arranged as galleries in a museum. After hard work it is harder to resist temptation.

Placing her things outside the bedroom door, she opens it slowly, and puts her head round. It is a large, light-filled room with plain terracotta wallpaper and two windows looking out onto the street.

Bedrooms disappoint her with their lack of surprises and secrets. She stands by the neat bed, vainly cultivating the feeling of sex. Bedrooms should be different from other rooms, the wallpaper in them should be garish or tatty, the furniture chipped and mismatched, the bed overlarge and untidy. She knows she should not think this. In her experience bedrooms are decorated in the same mousy style as the rest of the house. It is very boring. Never has she been in a bedroom that didn't bore her. She longs for a bedroom to give her the shock of her life.

First she inspects the corners of the room, behind the door, down the side of drawers and behind the bedside cabinet. Next she gets down on her knees, making a slight *whumph* noise of effort, and looks under the bed. She sits up pensively. Then, rolling up her sleeves, she goes through the drawers of the dresser, the chest of drawers, the wardrobe, the bedside cabinets and the laundry basket, pulling up handfuls of underwear, handkerchiefs, socks.

No one knows what she suffers, she thinks. She takes off her glasses and wipes perspiration from her big face. Where has he put them?

It is the thought of anecdotes which bothers him. Nothing in the world is good or bad but thinking makes it so. His watch, which he can see if he cranes his neck to the left, tells him that he has been immobile for forty minutes. His erect penis knows no passage of time. At any moment his wife and parents-in-law will open the front door. All things considered, he does not think that he can explain the stockings or the brassiere or the suspender belt decorated with red roses.

As for the anecdotes, he remembers some of them: tales from Casualty. Men who turn up complaining of a pain in the rectum which is caused, the doctors discover after investigation, by a blood orange inserted into the anus. 'I must have sat on it doc, I don't remember.' Men who arrive with their genitalia enmeshed in a vacuum cleaner attachment. 'I was sitting in my dressing gown reading a book, and my wife was doing the cleaning. She's a very clumsy woman, my wife.' Michael has heard of a man who went to the hospital complaining of a pain in his penis, and when he was examined, the doctors found a safety pin inserted into his uretha which had opened. Michael turns these stories over in his mind. What sadness there is in the world that hilarity must be made from such tragedies: is it to stop us from weeping? Is dignity so much beyond us we must laugh at suffering?

In times of lethargy, cynicism and low comedy – the critics note – farce is the only mode of expression. We live in an Age of Farce. Michael concludes that our culture is doomed.

In a little while rain starts, crackling the leaves of the beech hedge. The light on the carpet alters, shifts. Through the half-opened window come the sour smells of vegetation and soil; and he listens and smells, entranced, thinking not of his predicament but of a rainstorm in Barcelona in the summer of 1987, the last year when he was really happy, rain warm and thick and relentless, stirring up the dust and smelling of rotten wood. It was his honeymoon. He lay on the bed next to his wife, listening to the rain and reading *Tristram Shandy*. But *was* it 1987? Or the year after, or the year after that? Surely he can remember the year he was married. He will have to check his book diary. Since he has been unemployed, time has become both more personal and more elusive, another part of him he cannot interpret.

The pursuit of happiness is another of his themes, but he will not think of it, it is too sad. Last night his wife had one of her nightmares, he woke at three in the morning to the sound of her informing him that snakes were getting into the car. She was sitting up in bed, hugging herself, one of her arms bare and hot against his shoulder and her hair messed across her face. There was a smell off her like overripe fruit. 'There aren't any snakes,' he whispered. 'They're not in the car, darling.' 'It's my fault,' she said in the same lost voice. 'I left the door unlocked. Snakes every-where. So many snakes.' He loves comforting her when she has nightmares, when she has a nightmare he is happy for a little while; he sits up and holds her, her hair in his face, the weight of her breasts in her night-dress on his arm; he rocks her softly saying, 'No snakes, there aren't any snakes.' Sometimes, when she is insistent, when he can't wake her, he says, 'Nice snakes, friendly snakes, going now, bye bye snakes, bye bye, all gone now.' And she sighs, still asleep, and settles down. Last night she woke quickly as he was speaking. 'I was having a nightmare,' she said briskly, interrupting him. 'That's all. Go to sleep.'

Nightmares are their only moments of intimacy.

His eyes refocus, and he sees his penis sticking out like a flaw in a fantasy.

Closing the door behind her, she goes out of the front gate and down Parkside Road, and immediately feels the beauty of the day. The rain has stopped and the sky is bright and the air feels hot. It is July, after all. Parkside is lovely and banal. She tells herself, without resentment, that she will deliver the League of Young Evangelists' leaflets, and overhead suddenly in the strongly-coloured blue and white sky a balloon appears and drifts away and is lost behind the rooftops, a diminishing silver speck. She walks on. Blackbirds and starlings stab and twitch, staking out the gravel beds, the miniature ponds, the bathroom-rug-sized lawns, the cracked concrete. You would not think there was so much variety in the front gardens. She thinks with satisfaction: some people don't know how to look after what they've got, some people ruin it with attention. The Ainslings' hydrangea has been cut back too severely again, the gate is still not properly fixed. Sighing, she lets herself in.

On the blue tiled work surface in the kitchen there is a pile of wrinkled clothes and two notes folded in half. One has 'Janine' written on it, the other 'Michael'.

She reads: *Janine please would you wash the kitchen floor today and do the windows. If Michael has put a new plug on the vacuum cleaner then please hoover the hall and stairs. There's laundry in the linen basket and ironing here. The bins need emptying. The bathroom needs a clean. You don't seem to have done the dusting in the front room for a while. Thank you.*

Then she reads: *THE HOOVER STILL NEEDS A PLUG. It needs to be done BEFORE JANINE GETS HERE. Water the garden. Shopping. Ring the DHSS. Janine please don't read notes left for Mr Ainsling.*

'Janine,' she says out loud, 'please don't read notes left for Mr Ainsling.' Her owlish reflection sits in the centre of the dirty window which she must clean. All she wants is to be shocked. Anger is no substitute.

For a moment she considers Mr and Mrs Ainsling. Why does he put up with her? She is a snob and a bully, her clothes are too tight, her face is always too heavily made up. He is kind. Of course his clothes are childish — T-shirts, jeans with elasticated belts, training shoes with the tongues missing — and he is perhaps not too bright, smiling too readily and uneasily, nodding his head and apologising, or asking her opinion and not listening to her answer. But he is kind. And she, Mrs Ainsling, is cruel.

Could it be sex? she asks herself.

Thinking this, she goes through the kitchen, through the incomplete extension, into the garden.

The noise of the latch startles him out of his dreams, and he flinches with a whimper, listening to the buckling of the key in the lock, the scrape of the door opening, the whump as it shuts. But the footsteps on the floorboards of the hall are not his wife's, they are too reticent and stolid. How often, he thinks, has he been taken by surprise at crucial moments, anticipating one thing and suddenly struck helpless by another? It is a law of his life, he thinks; it is the way he lives. His wife would have a thing or two to say about crucial moments, about surprise, about helplessness. He tries to remember the passage in Bellow's *The Dean's December* in which the Dean goes to sleep with his hands cupping his wife's breasts.

Intruding into his thoughts suddenly comes a voice from downstairs singing out an odd, mocking phrase, and he remembers the girl who comes to clean. It is too late to announce himself ('I'm busy at the moment Janine, can you leave the upstairs till next week?'), and he imagines her taking fright at the mere sound of his voice. She is a pasty, prudish girl, overweight and obsessed with sex; and he is always, unreasonably, kind to her. Why, he wonders, should he be kind to a girl he barely knows and has no liking for, when he often fails to be even polite to his wife whom he loves, whom he adores, after whom he lusts? Why such lavish normality with the cleaner when his domestic life is a travesty? His despair is so deep it is almost erotic, he is consumed by images of his wife, his desirable, indifferent wife. He even touches his penis again, but sadly, as if they must part. His penis aches with being erect. His back aches with being bent over. What must he do to get his wife's attention? Lately she is out a lot, she visits, shops, makes conversation, and he stays at home and reads, or wanders round Parkside feeling the air saturated with women and their babies.

It can't go on. He knows his marriage is failing – emotionally, biologically, in all ways it is falling into disrepair. Recently his wife has had a number of appointments at the hospital; the doctors say that they will not be able to have more children. His wife talks of therapy, of counselling, but as if these are inevitable late stages in the terminal decline of their relationship.

It is raining again, he hears it stirring the leaves like a lament, and he realises, with tears in his eyes, that it is far too late to alert the cleaner, twenty minutes have passed since she arrived. He will share a fate with his penis, he thinks: farce, humiliation and madness.

Lowering her face from the sun she sips her coffee and appraises the expensively laid-out garden which does not fool her. The lawn is a welter of bald patches and clover; the clematis which was growing across the chestnut pole arch has been allowed to die; bindweed is strangling the buddleia; the bird bath of weathered granite is listing badly and will soon collapse into the rose bed. Sometimes it is difficult not to see everything as a struggle between good and evil.

In one direction she sees the Parkside back gardens, a clothes-line in each, as if the extensions were tethered to the trees; and in the other the church, salmon pink in the sun. She thinks of singing and bells and the leaflets she must post, but when she has finished her coffee she goes back inside and reads the article in the paper about the peeping Tom.

Thirty-three-year-old Vincent Maclehose was yesterday found guilty on eight counts of lewd behaviour and was ordered to do ten hours a week community service. The court heard how he pestered sixth-form girls at St Thomas's School, following them home and making obscene suggestions. Twice he exposed himself. On the Friday before the Bank Holiday, Maclehose, who resigned his position in the cashiers department of the county office in December and has since been unemployed, was apprehended on the school premises hiding in a tree overlooking the gymnasium. He had with him a telescope and claimed to be a bird spotter. Mr Laxness, who teaches PE at St Thomas's, chased him across the school grounds and succeeded in locking him in a shed used for storing winter sports equipment where the police eventually apprehended him. The court was told that Maclehose had also confessed to entering a number of houses at night in order to watch girls as they slept. The plea of not guilty on the grounds of diminished responsibility, submitted by the defence, was not admitted.

Staring into the dirty window, biting her lip and winding her hair round a finger, she tries to bring to mind obscene suggestions. Sometimes her thoughts are so crude she can't imagine how she came to think them, and she quickly thinks instead of the floor that needs washing, the leaflets of the League of Young Evangelists that need posting, the teachings of her church on matters of grace, temptation and retribution. It seems to her that her real life is elsewhere, and she stands at the edge of it, waiting for the nudge that will either readjust her or send her over the edge.

In the bathroom he briefly takes an interest in his erection and its astounding longevity, but the discomfort of his position is acute, and he feels a headache coming on. If only he could go and lie down on the bed with the curtains half-drawn, as he usually does. He'd pick up the book he was reading – Ovid's *Metamorphoses* – and prop it on his chest until he fell asleep. The Ovid is the Melville translation, a World's Classics edition with the reproduction of Veronese's languid *Venus and Adonis* on the front cover. 'Of bodies changed to other forms I tell,' etc. But, of course, the real subject is the petty violence and outrageous tenderness of love.

Part of his day he spends reading, part napping,

and part snooping round the house. Snooping is his prime version of the pursuit of happiness; in the hour before lunch, after he has finished checking the paper and making phonecalls, he wanders into a randomly-chosen room and imagines something is hidden there. What? Something he has never seen before, something he can't define, a detail to redeem the whole perhaps, to make his wife love him again. Instead, of course, he finds what he already knows, familiar things, consolations. But consolation is important, he thinks. Minutiae from the past excite him: a packet of birthday cards, an album of wedding photos, old notebooks, clothes his wife no longer wears.

This morning, in a suitcase discovered on the top shelf of his wife's wardrobe, he found things from his honeymoon. Underneath an assortment of objects, all of which produced dim, lovely memories (such as a water bottle made from ribbed milk-white plastic with an acid-green cap from which he and his wife had drunk when they hired bicycles to ride to Sitges), were two outfits of black lace underwear which he didn't remember at all. For half an hour, with the underwear in his hands, he sat on the bedroom floor, trying to remember what his wife had worn at night in Barcelona, and then he put on one of the outfits, it seemed the natural thing to do.

Suddenly he hears footsteps on the stairs. In panic he sees himself as the cleaning girl will see him in a moment, a sort of big, frightened, almost-bald bird with a few patches of badly-fitting plumage trying to bury its head in the carpet. This is his fate. His fate is the whim of a wit or retard.

But the footsteps go past the bathroom door, along the landing and into the main bedroom. Opening his eyes, he discovers that he is clutching his penis again, not erotically, but for comfort and support – they are both in this together after all – and to his astonishment he wants to laugh, he has to put the back of his hand into his mouth to stop himself.

The kitchen floor has been washed, the windows are clean, the bins have been emptied, the living room dusted, and in a fury she goes up the stairs, across the landing and into the bedroom.

The Ainslings' bedroom is a mess but it is not the chaos of erotic love. This bedroom is not *the* bedroom, she tells herself. There's a book on the unmade bed, a scattering of toys on the carpet (spinning top, Pinocchio with a broken foot, damp rabbit) and, under the far window, a suitcase with the lid up. But wait. From where she stands she sees that the suitcase is full of underwear, black lace, frills, erotic lingerie, and she starts towards it with her mouth opening. She can hardly believe it. It *is* the bedroom, after all.

The underwear is expensive, black lace decorated with red roses. Her chest tightens. Amazed, she fits the knickers over the palm of her big hand, pulling them slightly down, then slightly up, then slightly to each side in a rotary motion in order to examine them from every angle, and then before she has a chance to enjoy them, she is looking queasily about her, saying, 'Oh no, oh *no*!' and running to the window. 'Please God,' she says to herself. What retribution is this? But there is no doubting the knickers which she holds up to the light. It can't be, she thinks, but it is. It is a familiar pair of black lace knickers decorated with red roses. It is the underwear she found in Mr Polunin's bedroom. It is Mr Polunin, semi-naked and unbearably agitated, and Mrs Ainsling in her black lace writhing like a teenager on his neat burgundy duvet. It is the shock of her life – at last.

Belligerently, she stands misting up the bedroom window. Should she pray? She has never felt less like praying. The thought of Mr Polunin and Mrs Ainsling is disgusting, but she is outraged above all by herself, her reflection in the misted windowpane like a bystander – mouth open, hair round her wide face like pencil scrawl – and she turns and runs towards the bathroom, feeling the nausea rise. Halfway along the landing she falls against the banisters but staggers forward and grabs the door handle.

Dignity is his great theme. It is natural for him, agonisingly incapacitated in his bathroom, dressed in articles of his wife's underwear, in a state of permanent arousal, with his wife about to return home and the cleaning girl working her way through the house towards him, to consider dignity. His wife in particular has always told him he has none.

The conclusion he reaches is that dignity relates to suffering. Suffering must be involved, it seems.

Without suffering dignity is impossible. So we have the Stoics, the itinerant friars with their begging bowls, the martyrs, lesser and greater. We have Michael Ainsling in his bathroom.

It is not his wife's pity he wants, he tells himself.

Sudden footsteps interrupt his reflections, thumping along the landing from the bedroom. There is a cattle-sized crash which makes him flinch, then more footsteps, louder still if possible, and finally a violent tug on the door handle.

At once, without thinking, he begins to whistle.

On the other side of the door there is a brief but very loud scream, then silence. He wants to laugh but it is only terror. With his hands held protectively over his groin, just in case, and his forehead on the washbasin lip, he squeezes his eyes shut and tries to control himself. Although he knows he should speak to the girl who is now presumably in a state of shock, if possible offer a few words of explanation, invent something at least, nothing comes to mind; and it is anyway too late to reveal himself, it would be certain humiliation. So he is silent, almost holding his breath.

After a moment he hears the girl speak. 'You better not come out of there,' she says. She naturally assumes him to be capable of movement.

There is a long pause after this. He decides not to whistle again, but he cannot rid himself of the urge to giggle.

'You better stay in there,' she says. 'I've got something and I'll use it.' This is hilarious: he bites the back of his hand. Her voice is shockingly aggressive but somehow enticing, as if perhaps she is trying to start a conversation.

He can hear her retreating slightly, back towards the stairs.

'I'll scream,' she says. 'They all know I'm here.'

After a moment there are more footsteps, and when she speaks again her voice is louder, as if she has come back to stand outside the door, compelled by curiosity or rage. 'You bastard,' she whispers. 'I knew it was you all along.' And then he hears her thumping downstairs.

Between pity and lust there is a middle ground, he thinks: a particular sort of love – of both violence and tenderness – and this is what he wants, this is what will do for him and his wife.

Startled out of her wits by the obscene noise in the bathroom, and finding herself near the top of the stairs frozen in an attitude of alarm, one arm flung out and one hand over her mouth, she can't stop herself wondering what sort of impression she will make on the sex attacker when he emerges. Glancing at her egg-shell blue outsize ski-pants and scarlet cotton T-shirt, she sees Mrs Ainsling's black lace knickers in her outstretched hand and staggers sideways with the horror of this, but freezes again when she hears another noise in the bathroom, oddly muffled, as if – she thinks – the pervert might be hiding among the towels.

Silently cursing the League of Young Evangelists

whose leaflets she will definitely not deliver, she tells herself that she will never be the same again. If this is retribution she accepts it.

Mumbled apologies, apparently, come from the other side of the door, and as the exhilaration of terror dissipates she becomes sceptical. Could it all be a joke? Frightened and disappointed at the same time, she winds her hair around a finger and glares at the door.

'Come out of there,' she hisses. There is no answer; the only sound is her own breathing, harsh and loud, as if she were a weight-lifter snorting air into her lungs before the assault on the barbells. 'No man would look at you twice,' her sister had said. But her sister has never been sexually assaulted

'You better not come out,' she shouts. 'I've got a knife, and I'll use it,' she adds, and actually examines her hands, as if by chance she's telling the truth.

'I'll scream,' she threatens almost immediately, remembering that she has not mentioned this, but her whole performance is beginning to disappoint her. Furious, she marches to the door as if to fling it open it, but stops and surprises herself by hissing, 'Don't think I don't know who you are. I knew it was you all along.' And then she is running downstairs.

The glans of his penis has turned a violent mulberry colour as if in shame. Nothing will ever be the same again: it is as if he had stepped out of his skin and confronted himself from the other side of the door. Still, even in extremis, he cannot concentrate: his thoughts are self-consciously his thoughts, he cannot help thinking about himself thinking about what to do, just as he can never think of his wife without also thinking of his love for her. It is a puzzling part of him he will never solve. Already he has totally forgotten the cleaning girl, who was here just a moment ago.

What would it be, he thinks now, in the little time he has left, to make an inventory of his entire relationship with his wife, remembering everything in order, beginning with the first time he met her and ending with the present moment, as he prepares to meet her in their bathroom, crippled, priapic and dressed in her underwear?

He remembers the first time he slept with her. She made it clear that sex was out of the question. He remembers the frightening paleness of her skin, the taut fullness of her, the way she walked naked into the bed, flat-footed – as if her feet were unaware of her sexiness. Since that night he has been infatuated with her.

Sounds come up the stairwell, the cleaning girl letting him know that she is telephoning the police, and at the same time there is another noise suddenly, the front door opening and his wife, his son, and his in-laws arriving noisily for lunch. He can hear the uproar but it is remote and somehow off the point.

This is the moment, he is thinking to himself, that his marriage has been building towards, exactly this high point. He can't help smiling. There is a way of looking at it which makes it not a disaster after all but, on the contrary, the climax of his love for his wife. He has been transformed. When he thinks of the actual moment when his wife will open the bathroom door and see him crouching inside wearing her knickers, brassière and stockings – his erection pushing itself into the picture ('Me too! Me too!') – he thinks he will be the image of the violence and outrageous tenderness of love. The fiercer his love, the more wild-hearted his wife. Never again will she be indifferent to him, nor he to himself – married or divorced they will be bound together on a wheel of fire.

Downstairs there is an amount of screaming but he doesn't even hear it, he is laughing too loudly. Frankly taking hold of his penis, as if to steady himself, as if, without his penis to hold onto, the whole world might collapse, he laughs and laughs until the tears run down his face.

# POSTCARDS FROM XENOS

1. Xenos, smallest and nastiest of the Cycladean islands, a bubble in the boiling water of the Aegean. Have pity on this island, do not destroy it yet. Soon.

2. Beer froth like the lifeless surf of the Xenosian beach slides over the bar top into the man's lap. The man dressed in white cotton sports shirt and baggy shorts. Wet baggy shorts. His face ruddy, beard sun-bleached, eyes startling grey. Waving away my apologies, shouting to the barman, 'Cloth, cloth!' His hand held up (big rings, dirty fingernails). 'Before you go, Nikos, crème de menthe, make it a double.' His red face turning to me. 'This weather. Fah. Don't get this in Leatherhead. Where you from?'

3. Hotel Dionyssos. Of wine, of vegetation, of indifferent baklava, of interminable moussaka. A suffering god, of madness, death and resurrection; inspiring music and poetry; associated with tragedy, comedy, ecstasy and mysticism. His constant companions satyrs, sileni, maenads, bassarids and the like. Enjoys perfect sea front position, enviable seclusion, prompt access to Xenos Town. Overlooks gardens (solemn strip of

coarse grass chequered with concrete patios), com-
pound of orange and yellow plastic sunbeds (rearing
their heads like gaudy salamanders), beach (golden,
virgin, etc.), the Aegean – the edge and cradle of
civilisation. The season of '92, August, the rage of
tourist magazines. Evening. Heat despite the absence
of sun. The air stiff. 'Fah,' he repeats. 'This weather.'
Grinning. He says, 'You've caught it.' I lift my hand
to my cheek and see him look at my ring, and
look round.

4. Heat wave too hot even for Greeks – the subject
of our halting conversation. The woman approaches,
fortyish, sunburned. She has shoulder-length blonde
hair and a narrow face, lined, as if the fine structure
has begun to crack after so much use. She says, 'What's
this, Paul?' 'What's what?' he says. She says, 'Never
crème de menthe before dinner, what am I always
telling you?' 'Never crème de menthe?' he says. She
says, 'Oik. You're an oik.' Saying to me, 'He knows,
don't think he doesn't know.' Saying to him, 'Senile,
darling, I think you're going senile.'

5. Playing with my ring. I note that he has several
rings, she none. Scenting adultery, for no reason, as
they bicker.

6. I say, 'I have an awful memory,' and both turn to
look at me as if they have never seen me before. A
double meaning in my statement. They do not know
how utterly mad I am.

7. 'Liz!' Sharp as a dog trainer. 'Here!' She says, 'What's this now?' 'Ouzo,' he says. She says, 'Ouzo, Paul?' 'It's what this lot drink,' he says. Pause. She says, in anguished tones, 'Oh God, give me a real man, give me one who knows about things, get me away from this one.' Laughter . . .

8. One hour later. Shadows in the garden. (Of paradise, of expulsion.) Colours draining from sky and sea, merging together, grey. Heat despite all this. Bouzouki music from the stereo, smell of burned-up sun-oil on skin, of fried fish from the dining room. Still we drink. Sweating still, on white vinyl bar seats, bare (sunburned) thighs unsticking with a smacking kiss. This is what we are about: facts and the illusion of facts. When on holiday this irrepressible urge to autobiography. Paul and Liz work together. Have I ever heard of Brightwell's, exemplary manufacturer of machines for the food industry? Of course not. I say, 'Brightwell's? Yes, of course.' She is a secretary, he is in sales. Once they were married to other people; they had an affair (days remembered of motorways in his untrustworthy car, of her caustic humour in the typing pool); now, divorced, they live together. She says, 'We don't get on at work, never did. I thought he was an oik. Still is, aren't you, darling?' 'We hate each other,' Paul says. 'She's a real bitch, you would not believe.' She says, 'It's hard, it's just hard.'

9. She says, 'I don't suppose you work with your wife? Too sensible.' We all look together at my ring,

the bouzouki music accelerating, straining to break through to a tune we all know. She says, 'Aren't I nosy?' I smile, I say, 'My wife's dead.' It doesn't come out right, it never does I suppose. There's a sudden, confused silence, as after an unexpected Latin tag. 'You and your big mouth,' Paul says. 'Nosy cow, what are you?' She says, 'I wasn't to know, I didn't mean to upset him.' 'Can't keep it shut for a second,' he says. 'You're like one of those wind-up things.' She says, 'When I talk I've got something to say.' 'Talk, talk, talk, it's indecent,' he says. She says, 'Don't talk to me about indecent.' I tell them that it's difficult to get off, and they turn to me with astonishment, as if a total stranger materialised in their midst. 'The ring,' I say. 'It's difficult to get the ring off.' Holding up my hand, all looking together at my ring.

10. The cardiac bouzouki terminates. Fish-smells overpowering. A pause gathering momentum, a polite attendance on the narrative, the suspicion dawning that they want more. I give them more: a wet night, a skidding car, the rush to hospital, an operation, complications, a coma, the final seconds, the passing spirit. A yelp of buttock on vinyl. Liz asks, 'How old was she?' Paul moans. She says, 'I'm not being nosy, you.' Paul moans. I am about to tell her twenty-seven, I tell her twenty-one. Tears in her eyes. Unsticking herself from her seat, she embraces me silently, my elbows on her breasts, her breath sweet but harsh, my gaze squashed towards the ceiling, as the bouzouki starts up once more, in

triumph. 'Jeremy, oh Jeremy,' she says. She does not know how mad I am. This is the nature of secret lives: the sticky air, the squashed breasts, the yelp of vinyl.

11. Night again. An impression of nearby (promptly accessed) Xenos Town: daemonic cocktail bars, night-marish greasy-spoon cafes and curry houses, discos throbbing like the war-drums of marauding armies. In the dark, on the hot, deserted roof of the Dionyssos Hotel, I sit watching my wife. In the ophthalmic circle of the telescope she appears, like Aphrodite, with her lover, there on the balcony of their room at the Hotel Priapus fifty yards away. It is not called Priapus. A splash of electric light, very festive. Glints off a bottle, better and better. The mind circling hesitantly round details. Her red hair across her shoulders . . . her face . . . her T-shirt . . . her breasts . . . I think they are her breasts. She leans forward to put her hand on her lover's knee. I think it is his knee. And now, without a bow, the protagonists leave; a slight whoosh of the curtains and the balcony is empty. Secret lives, secret loves. I glance at my watch. Last night exactly the same.

12. Truth is a cuckold with his eye to the end of a telescope. For him everything is true. A week now I've been in Xenos spying on my wife who has come here on a romantic holiday. Ex-wife. Six months ago she left me for the man on the balcony: solicitor, athlete, retard. She met him at her aerobics class. Where else do you meet these types?

13. I have a plan; I have no plan. I have no wife.

14. An impression of this attic room: sweltering rough concrete, walls and ceiling striped with seams like scars from an operation – staff quarters leased to me at the last minute, at full-price, such my desperation. Where is the staff? Sleeping in ditches, hedges, on beaches, pavements. On their iron-frame bed I lie, breathing . . . not air, not air proper, not air as we know it, but air solidified, air like foam-rubber, air like the miasma of all my weary rage, into which I put my fist, splash, and move it weakly about. Discos pound distantly through two o'clock, three o'clock, four, five . . . This my hell of abandonment.

15. Morning stings, thrusting forward an overbright, colourless scene: bleached beach and mirror-bright bay. Six o'clock: the last karaoke singers and disco dancers have just fallen silent. Everything is quiet and stale, except for the coruscating sun. I swim into glare, slowly, keeping my head absurdly high above the wavelets, disliking water in such quantity, disliking the sun. Nothing ahead of me. To my left and right, if I turn my craning head, the horns of the bay materialise out of the morning mist, like thoughts hardening into fact. Swimming back towards the beach, the sun behind me now, the water appears darker, more agitated, billowing around me like sheets of silk. It is impossible to impose my own rhythm on the unpredictable rhythm of this sea.

16. At noon, sitting on the roof with my telescope, I am surprised by Paul and Liz, they emerge from a metal door with a clang. Liz says, 'We didn't know where you were.' Before I can drop the telescope over the edge of the roof they have seen it. Liz says, 'What are you doing with that telescope?' 'Will you stop asking him questions,' Paul says. 'It's driving me mad.' She says, 'He doesn't mind.' 'You say he doesn't mind,' he says. 'I don't mind,' I say. She says, 'Are you a bird watcher?' 'Christ!' Paul says. She says, 'Leave us alone, don't bully us, we're just talking.' Paul sighs. 'Here, let's have a go,' he says. I tell her I am a bird watcher. 'Useful for crumpet,' Paul says, scanning the beach. She says, 'I don't know why I bother.' Stroking his back, her blouse falling open. They want me to go with them to see a church along the coast. They are insistent. She says, 'I keep telling him there's more to Greece than tits. He doesn't care. I thought you'd be interested in churches. You look like you'd be interested in churches.' Nodding vaguely, looking away from her opened blouse.

17. If I had a plan I would be happy. If I had more time. (If I had a wife.) No plan, no time, but I run down the stairs, hot air grating on my blistered face, my raw arms; seeing myself as I go, a running sunburn, dull red. If I were decisive or aggressive I would be happy, I would not be sunburned, nor would I be running down the stairs; but I am even-tempered, cautious, given to sudden panic; the combination of things that is me is truly depressing. Through the lobby

into the garden ablaze, down the sand-strewn garden path to the beachside café where he sits at a table, drinking beer and reading a paper, legal in character no doubt. 'Hello,' I say. I think, 'Are you that bastard, the seducer of my wife?'

18. The fawn head bobbing up, surprised. 'Mind if I join you?' I say, teeth, spit and polish. Blue eyes flicking towards other, empty tables. 'Yes, you, you dozy bastard,' I think. He says, 'Help yourself.' He has a voice of suave assurance, thick neat hair (for clients), smooth face, hairless big-muscled legs (for aerobics, jazz-dancing and sexual athletics). 'What are you drinking?' I say. 'Bring this man a dish of his own urine,' I think. He says, 'Amstel actually.' I say, 'Think I'll have the same. Another?' He smiles: wide mouth, lots of teeth. 'Kind of you,' he says. 'Very kind,' he says. Not knowing kindness in all its forms of savagery. 'Marcus,' he says finally, putting out a hand. 'Conrad,' I say. 'Your nemesis,' I think. I say, 'Nice to meet you Marcus.'

19. Twice a week for approximately three months (I compute), on the pretext of attending a night class on Modernism in European Literature, my wife met this fawn, big-muscled man at an aerobics class she went to in the hope of picking up men. He knows nothing of Woolf, of Mann, of Ibsen, of Joyce, of Eliot, of Proust, of Pirandello, of Kafka. Nothing of Conrad. His eyes shaded, watchful on the progress of my wife in the sea, that seal, her head tilted back as if pulled

by the hair — her hair, her red hair spread out on the water like a slick of blood. How I love her hair. I say, 'Where are you from, Marcus?' He drops the name. 'Parkside?' I say. He says, 'Oh, do you know it?' 'No, no, never heard of it,' I say. Fighting down the mad urge to cackle. 'Nice place?' Parkside, house-prices, careers, special deals on Greek hotels facilitated by one's partners — these are the main themes of our imbecilic conversation. Big, he is big, but boyish, as if he shot up suddenly overnight. A red slick drifts ashore, bobbing closer.

20. 'Fancy another?' He says this, not knowing what he says. I say, 'No thanks, I'm going in for a swim, keep fit.' 'Know what you mean,' he says. I say, 'You look as if you keep yourself pretty fit.' I think, 'It's the fucking, isn't it, the constant fornication?' 'Aerobics,' he says. Another cackle choking me. 'Go twice a week back home.' He sneezes onto the table. 'With the girlfriend. Met in an aerobics class would you believe.' Looking at me interrogatively. I say, 'My wife's asleep, she's asleep in our room, she needs a lot of sleep. That's my wife.' He says, 'We should get together, I know this really good place on the coast.' I am about to vomit. I say, 'She sleeps a lot, in the evening, she needs a lot of sleep.' 'Is she pregnant?' he asks. 'No,' I say furiously. 'Not pregnant, not pregnant at all.' 'Marriage, hmm,' he says ruminatively, and cynically laughs. I smile politely. What is the bastard thinking of? Not my madness, which is what he should be thinking of. Following his eyes, I see my wife wading

like a titan through the waves, adjusting the strap of her bikini, a terrifying detail I'd pay to avoid, rubbing water from her eyes, knee-deep in sand-cloudy sea, her legs churning up foam, swaying, almost losing her balance, suddenly appearing so vulnerable it is as if she has slipped back in time, as if she needs me to hold on to, and I take an involuntary step seaward. But her elbows stab powerfully upwards as she recovers her balance and she comes blindly on again, ploughing water. Aerobics, aerobics, the lost world of the gods.

21. Quiet, cool, dark in church, the silence disturbed only by Paul. He whispers, 'What's this for then? Look at that. Small or what, these Greeks must have small bums to sit on these.' Rebuilt after the earthquake of 1953, decorated with modern icons, the church lacks all style, shape or sense. Crass murals dominate, the saints swarthy, elaborately bearded and sleekly confident of heaven. John the Baptist giving a double look of *hauteur*, once from the head on his shoulders, once from the head on a plate at his feet. How to get what you want. Drastic politics of martyrdom.

22. The hotel bar is brighter and more apathetic. Paul says, 'Reminded me of English summer, that church. Dark and cold.' He laughs for a while, then becomes sad. 'Be home soon anyway.' 'I liked the church,' I say. Liz says, 'I liked the church too, we like the same things.' Paul says, 'Small bums, those Greeks have.' He says, 'Tell you what, before we go we ought to go to that restaurant, that place on the coast, what's

it called, Sunset Taverna, hire scooters or something, see the sunset.'

23. Morning again. Sitting watching my wife's balcony until six. Then going for a swim, and floating on my back, my head craning out of the water, looking shoreward to see the row of white hotels stacked like packing crates against blue sky, white and blue, the Greek national colours. By just closing my eyes I can turn everything red, the colour of my dreams.

24. She complained, my wife, of being overweight. With her round arms, her hefty shoulders, her boneless lilt. With her imploring, vague look, as if she did not know what she wanted. With her heavy eyelids that gave her the sleepy look of a cat, a creature used to the dark. With her habit of running her hands through her hair, turning her face away, as if concealing some momentous, some erotic secret. I did not know her, that's why I loved her, I did not know who she was, she was a stranger. Then she changed; even I noticed. It all started with European Modernism. She lost weight, her legs clenched, her hips tightened. I knew her then. She became powerful, she dug the air with her elbows when she walked, tough and efficient, the walk of someone who knows what she wants, what she does not want.

25. Sitting in the hotel garden dreaming of violence when Marcus appears. Trying to duck behind a bush with a cramped lurch. Marcus looking down at me.

I say, 'Did you see it, a Large Turquoise, gone now. Butterflies, my hobby is butterflies.' He says gravely, 'You've been overdoing it, Conrad.' He does not know, however, how much. He examines my blisters and scabs, the burned detritus of my skin. He says, 'You don't use sun oil. You should, actually. You can use mine if you like, you can't trust the muck you get out here.' I say, 'Oh, I'm fine. Fine, thanks. It's only pain.' 'I came round to buy you the beer I owe you,' he says. I say, 'What, now?' 'Yes, now, why not?' he says. To be wary is to be safe, is to maximise your chances of survival. I say warily, 'I wouldn't want to intrude.' Expansively he says, 'The girlfriend's gone shopping. Bit of peace.' Looking round the garden, looking at me. I say, 'My wife's in bed, she's sleeping, she needs a lot of sleep.' Surreptitiously looking at my watch. Behind a plane tree a cicada begins to thrum, accents of antiquity, of death, betrayal and catharsis. Whose plan is this?

26. Marcus talks. Of women: a rapid and theoretical analysis. Marcus dimpled, Marcus boyish, Marcus wry. My head swivels, on the lookout for a glimpse of red hair. He says, 'How long have you been married, Conrad?' 'It depends,' I say warily. He says, 'What, what did you say?' Shaking my head, mumbling, often finding it best to mumble. 'Marriage,' he says. I say, 'Call it what you like.' He talks. Of marriage: a lengthy, Hogarthian account which will end, I see, in a confidence. 'Can I confide in you, Conrad?' he says. I nod gravely. 'Everything you say,' I think, 'will

be used against you.' The story is this: his girlfriend wants to get married. She's been married before, but she wants to get married again, the marriage was a disaster. A mad grin appearing on my face, like an inflammation, like a boil. He says, 'Time to part company. I'll be telling her in a night or two actually, thought I'd take her to that Sunset Taverna, nice backdrop, poignant actually. Want to come? I won't tell her till the end, needn't spoil a nice meal.' I know how mad I am, but he doesn't. I am going to be sick, and Marcus doesn't know that either. Still discoursing on women and marriage, undigested Amstel swills across the table into his lap, like flood waters, like the Day of Judgement, and I fall off my chair.

27. Sun going down, invisible, in grey haze, is not in any routine sense of the word a sunset. The silence of disappointment is broken only by staccato chatter of oblivious waiters moving rapidly among tables al fresco, among glum diners with their unused cameras, light-meters, wide-angle attachments, tripods and cam-corders. This is the silence of oblivion, of half-posterity after the old gods have died, and before the new ones have burned into consciousness. My knees are still bleeding from the scooter ride. It is with machinery I have problems, with machinery and people. Liz says, 'How long ago was it, Jeremy, I mean the bereavement?' 'For God's sake, no questioning,' Paul says. 'You're worse than the bloody Spanish Inquisition.' She says, 'What do you know about

the Spanish Inquisition, ignoramus?' 'Lived with one for the last four years,' he says. She says, 'We're having a conversation. Eat your moussaka. Look at the sunset.' 'Bloody joke that is,' he says. 'If we were in England we could get them on the trades descriptions.' Waving to a waiter, shouting. She says, 'He always wants everything perfect, it must be why I love him.' Putting her hand on his thigh. Elegant fingers, chipped varnish.

28. Knowing nothing, believing nothing, affecting nothing, assuaging nothing, leaving everything undone. Plan? Hah!

29. In the hotel bar: the parting, the exchange of addresses, formal as diplomacy. Paul is cheerful. He says, 'Back to the bloody rain, back to the bloody British economy, bloody marvellous.' 'Take care of yourself,' she says, moist-eyed, beautiful, ageing into a massive compassion. As if we would weep. I have not been so stupid as to give them my real address. Do they think I'm mad?

30. I have no wife but I have a plan, I have a false moustache fashioned from a goatskin purse bought at the bazaar, and a floppy sunhat to conceal my face.

31. Tonight my wife is wearing tight white trousers, and a lemon elasticated tube which squashes her breasts across her chest, and nothing else. I could detect nothing else. My mission is to rescue my wife

from these clothes, from this absence of clothes. This is however the eighth disco this evening, on this mission, encountering so far, as usual, only noise apparently generated by the heat, darkness spasmodically lit by disco-lights, people with burned faces whose eye orbits have been kept white by sunglasses, woven straw roofs, and the jumping clientele. This is also my eighth cocktail. Down the steps I go wobbling to the beach to find motorbikes and people lying two to a sunbed, flowing figures with the pump of music ebbing over them, and moonlight on the bay making a snail's trail out to sea into which my whispering cocktail glass falls with a splash, echoed by someone's half-hearted cry: 'Hey!'

32. Morning again. It keeps coming around, there's no stopping it, or me, teeth gritted, swimming into the six o'clock sun, and those jags of black and green winking on the water, snake-shapes of light too quick to focus on. Here's a thing: if I stop swimming, I must tread water to avoid sinking. Would I be capable of stopping, of sinking? It seems improbable, I could stay afloat for hours, wanting to sink perhaps, not sinking, treading water, eventually turning shoreward again, and going on living. Much better to plunge from a great height into the water, stun myself, be flung against rocks, end it that way. Impaled like a constellation on the horns of the bay. Jeremy Wilson beloved of the gods, made mad and put to death. So I paddle shoreward again, looking this way and that, to where the horns protrude. But now that

they are visible, one of them is clearly detached, not a peninsula but an island, no longer a part of the mainland, but separate, separated perhaps in an earthquake, or an emotional upheaval. What was once joined now sundered.

33. So in its allotted time, the sun is declining, setting, like all suffering things. Concealed amongst dusty shrubs at the side of the road, I wait in my outsize motorcycle helmet and goat moustache, astride the scooter I cannot control. The plan, it's the plan. At last! My wife and Marcus come phut-phut-phutting out of the car park into the almost-sunset while I crouch in my grotto, peering through drab, prickly leaves. They go. I count to ten. Then I burst from the bushes in a storm of engine noise. Then I am pitched sideways. Then I am flung forwards and backwards simultaneously. Then dragged back into the bushes. My knees bleed once more, my moustache drips from my nose. Why are there always these complicitous, necessary relationships, so violent, so marital, with machinery, with people? Like the bewildered goon on the vicious fairground ride, my head in its huge, domed helmet snapping back, I emerge from the bushes a second time and, despite all my efforts, accelerate powerfully into the hotel car park from which my wife and Marcus have just emerged.

34. There are few life forms more cunning or low than the jealous husband, and although I have lost them now, the ones I pursue in my cunning, nevertheless

I have plotted their route in advance, and know their easy ride, and know their glee – Marcus's false, my wife's embarrassingly true – and I know the sea glinting below the cliff-road, light flecking the waves with yellows and greens, sun spreading and dazzling as it falls, and I can drive with my eyes screwed almost shut, and my teeth gritted, and my knees scalding in the salt air, into the past. I am not mad for nothing.

35. Finale. Exulting, peering round my menu, goat revolving on my upper lip, I watch. At the other side of the taverna they eat, eyes glued to the horizon. The sun hesitates. The waiter greets me gaily like an old friend, shouting, 'So nice you come again, so nice.' Angrily drawing attention to my moustache, shrinking into the shadows, I order. 'Why you whisper?' he shouts. 'You want moussaka? You have moussaka also the last time, do you think we have nothing but moussaka?' Appealing laughingly to nearby diners. Turning in the opposite direction I whisper my order to one of the poles which supports the awning, whispering of wine, lots of wine, buckets of wine, and the puzzled waiter laughingly departs.

36. The sun hesitates. I too would prefer to hesitate on the verge of this extinction, it is not what I wanted, not entirely, but plans are plans, plans are made and executed under terms of strictest obligation.

37. Hesitating, but slipping, slipping and fading, fading without effects, without effects of any kind, without

even a secondary characteristic of what might loosely be termed a sunset, again, into the grey sea, the dull sun sets. Groans from the diners. Pity, above all, for my wife, who has come so far to be so badly let down. Then her laughter rings across the restaurant, and I glimpse her, shadow gathering in her face like an illness. In front of me a wedge of moussaka sinks into itself, a dingy sunset, going cold.

38. The lighting of the candles, the ecclesiastical atmosphere, the requiem and the last rites. Suppose I did not know her, suppose that when that man with the fawn appearance leaves her weeping, I approach, concerned, or better yet, casual, and make a comment, a comment about something, about the sunset, the lack of sunset, and we begin again, or for the first time, and if I am the same, she is different, what then? I'm crying now into my retsina. 'Please,' says the waiter, eyeing my untouched moussaka. 'You don't like it? It makes you sad?'

39. Finales should not last so long.

40. Huddled over their brandies, looking for all the world like a married couple. And my second bottle of retsina half empty, swaying in my hand, as I look at my watch and grind my teeth.

41. Jerking upright. Staring wildly at deserted tables around. Have I been asleep? My wife and Marcus and everyone else have disappeared. My lap is wet.

Yes, wet! Who has done this? Which bastard? I am all action, thrusting my chair from the table, spraying gravel, thrusting myself after, hearing the waiter pounding behind – 'Please! Please!' – running back to the table, scattering money onto it – 'Yes! Yes!' – running away again. Then I am crouched panting over my scooter, that black, inexplicable shape in the shadow of, probably, a waiter's Seat, the door of which I kick, and kick again when the scooter won't start, before I hear voices, and plop to the floor, and stifle a squeal as my raw knees sink into the gravel.

42. Ten yards away on the cliff-edge sightseers' bench, they are sitting arguing. The backdrop of faint stars swims in and out of focus. First my wife's raised voice, then Marcus's tight, low one, then vice versa. Nothing audible, and then a sob, a suddenly flung something landing with a chink in the gravel nearby. My wife's extraordinary fury sharpened to this. Footsteps. A scooter roars, skids, slurs gravel, hurls a light backwards like an insult and is gone, gathering a tremendous noise into itself.

43. Marcus is sitting by himself on the sightseers' bench, in fresh silence, sighing, humming, crossing his legs and inquiring after another brandy. But why am I staring at him like this? The plan, where is the plan now I need it?

44. For the first time the scooter obeys me. It responds

to my drunkenness with effortless if disengaged flight down the black coast road. I have never felt so safe: beyond the hairpin bends lies the safety-net of the sea, a fine mesh of moonlight. The sound of slewing gravel at the blind side of the road, like the rattling of dice, is no other than the sensation of loss – the past rushing by like the air that rushes back against me, emptying me.

45. I buck against scrub on the cliff edge. Ahead my wife's scooter is careening downhill. The thought occurs: this is how it always was, the velocity, the syncopation of marriage. Her so-called betrayal means nothing, is over, did not exist. Plan? I would be happy to float over the edge, to be in love, to be love's martyr, love's buoy bobbing on the waves. I love it! I love my wife! I shout, toot my horn, take one hand off the handlebars and wave, wave. I'm not mad after all. Joyous. Joyous is the word.

46. Twenty yards ahead, she looks back and sees me. Tooting, shouting, waving. A funny thing happens. She speeds up.

47. Love's velocity, Love's momentum, Love's burning rubber; gravel thrumming, scrub bucking; Love's double helter-skelter. All smack into the air, the air where the road turns to sky.

48. Drawing alongside her, yelling, I yell, 'Me! It's me!' Clownlike, with a clown's great grin, I try to

take off my helmet to show her it really is me, she will not believe it otherwise, I know what she's like, my wife, she doesn't believe in miracles. Tears are streaming from my eyes. As I deal with this difficult manoeuvre. And she looks, looks aghast into my face, looking at me even as she skids sideways away with a thump and a scream, and jolts up once, high, and sits on the air like a bird, and vanishes.

49. Still hearing nothing but that scream of rubber, still seeing nothing but the slow whiplash of bends in the road still coming at me, I find myself somehow further on in the plot, on my knees, where I have always been, at the edge of the cliff, trembling, looking down and seeing nothing. The sea churning perhaps. It is dark. I can't be sure what has happened. What I've done. What I have not done. My thoughts are unclear. Are these angels bearing me up, or my raw knees? Did I do something? Was there something I missed? I was waiting for something to happen. Did it?

50. Water far below bulges out of darkness. This at least is familiar, this black and crowding immensity. And you? Love's martyr, Love's buoy, you are somewhere below. It's too late, after all, after all this, to take you in my arms and say wish you were here. It is very late and everything is beginning again.

# ENOUGH

## I

Our argument lasted twelve days, from the incident of the soap to the business with the smashed window, twelve days of insomnia and boredom and stifled tears. It took Wills that long to rouse himself to anger.

On the twelfth day we arrived back from holiday in Florida where we had been celebrating our ninth anniversary; it was near midnight, and we sat in the car with the engine off, looking at our house. The bay window was streaked with golden shadow from the street lamp, it seemed unfamiliar the way houses do after an absence, even a short one, begging awkward questions: Is this our house? Is this our style? Is this us? It was a beautiful night, faint clouds moving like breath across the bright stars. Hunched in his seat, deformed by his fury, Wills spoke. 'I've had enough,' he said. 'I want you out by the end of the month.' Then, as if shocked by what he had said, he fell silent. Too tired to laugh, I was silent as well, and the silence grew, and for half an hour we sat in the car, hugging ourselves, nursing our suntans against the English September air, looking into our separate reflections in the dark curve of the windscreen and seeing who knows what, perhaps images of the people we used to be or would become; and then we got out and went shivering to the back of the house where I smashed the window in the kitchen door with a flesh-coloured lump of limestone I pulled from the flowerbed next to the patio.

Wills and I met in 1980, at a small exhibition of pastels and water-colours held in a former farmhouse converted into an artist's workshop and gallery, in a village three miles south of the city. I had not been in England long, everything was new; I was disorientated by the countryside, the enigma of mist-hung water-meadows, the softness of wet, reddish earth, the spikiness of broom in the hedgerows. My friend, the artist, asked me if I had met Wills. 'You'll like him,' he said. 'Everyone likes him. He's the kindest man I know.' He brought him over and presented him to me as if he were one of his pictures, with a quick glance to see my first impression.

As sometimes happens, the party became distant, a vague noise behind me, and my friend drifted away, leaving me with this shortish long-headed man with a mole under his right eye and a large blunt nose. He was wearing a double-breasted grey suit and highly polished shoes, out of place among artists and groupies in ratty jeans and suede jackets. We talked about art; his voice reminded me of my mother's, soft but confident. He had a gay drawl with public school intonations, a surprising bubble of a laugh that in time I would learn to tease out of him and a habit of epigram. A painting, he said, should be like a person, capable of giving a terrific shock after years of uneventful intimacy. He was not handsome, he seemed to cultivate distance, as if he were keeping himself partly hidden; but in everything he said, in all his gestures and expressions, he seemed, as my friend had said, kindness personified.

The evening after we got back from Florida I cooked Fricassée Argenteuil and honey-baked French beans, and we sat in the kitchen eating out of the earthenware bowls we bought in Angoulême. After Wills's outburst, I had decided to carry on as normal.

Wills and I took our food very seriously. Food rated higher than either clothes or sex, and was exceeded only by interior decor. We used to drive out to farms to buy produce that still retained its taste, and thought nothing, on a routine day of the week, of spending two or three hours preparing a south Indian stew or Thai curry. We liked eating late. On the table there would be a bottle or two of wine, recommended by a journalist; on the stereo a Bach partita or Cole Porter. I am almost frightened, looking back, by our domesticity, by our small, civilised lives.

That evening even the kitchen seemed strange, and silence grew between us.

'I feel as if I haven't had a holiday,' I said at last. 'I feel holidayless.'

Wills said nothing. He pushed his food from one side of his plate to the other. We had given up wine for the week, and were drinking Evian.

'Next time,' I went on, 'I think Venice, or Paris. I don't want sun, I want paintings, buildings, the theatre.'

He blinked and swallowed, and said roughly, 'There is no next time. You'll be gone by then.' His face was grey with the extraordinary effort of his harshness.

Perhaps I had half-expected him to say something like this; even so I was shocked by the violence of his tone. And just as I was about to question him, just as I was about to say, 'Wills, what *is* all this?' he did an even more extraordinary thing: he got up from the table, overturning his chair and throwing down his napkin, left the kitchen and walked out of the house. The front door banged, and he was gone. He had eaten hardly any of his Fricassée Argenteuil.

I sat in the kitchen in silence. I sat there for *two hours*. Wills had undergone a sudden personality change. For twelve days, acting completely out of character, he had perpetuated a minor argument. Now he had capped it with an outburst of temper which I had not thought him capable of. I told myself: he isn't like this. I asked myself: how could I have thought I knew him? Finally, I could not believe it. But that's how it begins, with disbelief.

As I was going to bed the phone rang. It was a

student enquiring about the room for rent. He asked if I were the current lodger.

## II

The next day I stayed at home, unhappy and frightened to leave the house; I *clung* to it, knowing it was not mine. While Wills was out at work I went helplessly from room to room, sizing them up, not as prospective lodgers would soon size them up – for convenience, spaciousness and comfort – but for the quantities of memories that they contained. Before I properly knew what I was doing I had given myself over to remembering, to nostalgia.

I had moved into Wills's house about a month after the exhibition of pastels and water-colours. It was September, enormous clouds shifting slowly across hot skies, dead pine needles dropping from the trees in the park, smells of rust and diesel – the summer persisting in a long tranquil glow. Tentatively I made my mark on the house: I sat at windows, I lay on the beds and sofas, I went through cupboards and drawers, I used the lavatories, I paced up and down the garden. Isn't this how cats and dogs do it? I remember clearly sitting on a small two-seater sofa (long gone, but what did we do with it?) in the bay window, watching fractured sunlight slide off a yellow wall onto golden floorboards, thinking that whatever happened to me would be worth it. In all my life I had never felt such peace as I did in that strange house, such a sense of the unremarkable purpose of being alive.

I remember also that at first Wills was nervous, wary. Every morning he cycled into town to a large and ugly precinct (one modernist tower block, two low-rise laboratories and a short chain of offices) shared by the infirmary and the university where he ran the Disasters Studies programme as part of the Environmental Sciences curriculum; and when he left the house, around eight thirty, he gave me a very public kiss on the doorstep as if to teach me both his trust and the banality of his trust. I remember the way his face *actually tilted* with embarrassment when he put it up it to mine. But to his surprise, perhaps to mine too, I turned out to be trustworthy. In less than a month I had installed a garden-shed studio at the bottom of the garden and had begun work on the designs for stained glass decorations for the chapel of rest at the Ear, Nose and Throat Hospital. Art and Design impress people. I had several commissions. Wills's kiss became easier and less public. He introduced me to the neighbours.

He was a model neighbour. Whenever he saw a new family unloading their things from a removals van he would take them a pot of coffee and a plate of homemade Florentines or flapjacks, and introduce himself and ask if they needed anything. 'Hi, I'm Wills, I live with Nikos at number thirty-three,' etc. His voice, his gay frankness soothed them. The neighbours called us 'the boys'. We were even, I think, celebrated.

But if I am honest I will say that in my memories of Wills the large rites of arrival and possession and habitation are less vivid than the details of his physical appearance, and it is that long head I think of, that awkward face and blunt nose, those pale forearms, those sharp knees; his soft white hands (defenceless-looking, as if they had just been shelled); the seamed white scar on a thumb where a dog bit him when he was seven years old; his spatular toes with their broad grey nails; his thin dark hair; his tobacco-coloured eyes.

These are the things I am left with. But I wonder: do they add up? In my memories there are two versions of Wills, the kind and the unkind, and only one set of features. Who did they belong to?

# III

Looking back, I am amazed how orderly I was in my emotions: first unhappy, then indignant, finally angry. Wills would not talk to me, let alone explain himself, so I hypothesised reasons for his behaviour. One, he was unhappy and therefore confused; two, he was unhappy and therefore malicious; three, he was suffering from a psychosis and therefore irrational; four, he had fallen in love with someone else; five, he had fallen out of love with me. At the back of my mind was the vague and guilty fear that he had found out something about me, but I could not think what. Of all my hypotheses, I realised that the greatest pain would be caused by number four, so I believed it to be true.

On the second night back after our holiday I cooked Bouillabaisse Provençale for supper, and we sat in the kitchen, looking through the conservatory towards our little plot of lawn and flower-beds lit by concealed pearl-tinted illuminations installed the previous summer. We had contrived a Tivoli Gardens effect, despite the size of the garden. It was popular with the neighbours. The mauve and pink *millefeuille* of the sunset had given way to a bare pale sky like ash. I was drinking wine, Wills water. My behaviour was impeccable. The bouillabaisse was excellent.

'Wills,' I said at once, 'let's talk. What you've said, you've said. But I don't understand.'

He shook his head. I put my hand on his, and he withdrew it.

'Enough's enough, Wills. You have to explain it to me.'

He went grey-faced and threw down his cutlery.

'Don't you like the bouillabaisse, Wills?'

He began to make the effort to be nasty. His neck seemed to swell.

'Some things,' I said, 'I can still do.'

'After the end of the month,' he said, 'do them on your own.'

His shiftiness, his aggression, his tetchiness with the food were all ostentatiously unnatural. For an hour I questioned him, but all he would say was, 'It's over, it's just over.' A lie had never been more obvious nor so bare-faced. Over the course of the evening he became incredible to me, a creature I didn't know. He went into the sitting room and turned on the television, and I went with him, talking. He moved into the conservatory and sat next to the acanthus and picked up the paper, and I followed. By midnight a desperation, caused by my irrational conviction that I had done something to him, that he had found out something about me, possessed me and made me dangerous. I outlined my hypotheses, but they only aroused his irritation. All he would say, with great reluctance as if saying anything was an effort almost beyond him, was that our separation was inevitable. He seemed on the verge of leaving the house, as he had done the night before, as if he couldn't bear my company anymore.

In the end I became angry.

'Hypothesis number five,' I said. 'You don't love me anymore.'

He shrugged.

'And/or number four. There's someone else.'

He denied it.

'Is it because I'm untidy? Because I leave my clothes on the floor, because I don't screw the lid back on the jar of marmalade?'

'Not that.'

'Is it because I was silly about the soap.'

'It's nothing to do with the soap. Forget the soap.'

He would only say that our relationship had run its course. He was curt and rude.

'It's the sex, isn't it?' I said finally. 'You want

variety. I always thought you would turn into a dirty old man.' For some time I had been drinking the bourbon we brought back from Florida.

Suddenly he began to shout. Until that moment (I realised) I had never seen him angry, it was like watching him turn into a stranger. The stranger had a huge mouth, no chin and a thick vein throbbing in his neck.

'How many of them?' I asked him. I was near-hysterical. 'How *old* are they? Are they *legal*? Do they speak *English*?'

Wills walked up and down the conservatory, muttering, 'Get out! Get out!' the vein bulging and his ears moving.

'Let me guess,' I said, and also stood up. 'Number One is circumcised, he wears a thong, he calls you *Uncle*. Number Two . . .'

He stopped abruptly, near the Japanese box tree, and shouted, 'You whore!' He seemed to be disintegrating with the force of his anger. 'You *fag*!' he shouted. He was trembling all over.

'You're the one with boys,' I said. 'So who's the whore?'

That stopped him. Slowly he gathered together his dignity, and when he spoke it was in a quiet voice, much more like normal. 'Alright,' he said. 'Alright.' For a while he paced again, apparently thinking things through. Perhaps I'm wrong, but I think he actually wrung his hands. 'Alright, I admit it,' he said calmly. 'There is someone else.' He had stopped exactly in the middle of the conservatory, in the confluence of the lights, and his reflections stood in all the glass walls.

233

'I don't believe you,' I said quickly.

'You,' he added, with a look, 'have no right to ask me about it.'

'You're lying,' I said (ignoring this). I was off my chair and had adopted an aggressive position in the kitchen doorway.

'Now you know,' he said, looking round desperately. 'So you can stop asking me all these questions.'

We can all remember moments, situations, when our conversations seem made up not of words but of gestures. There is a point where words run out. I began to take off my clothes.

Wills watched me nervously from the conservatory. 'Nik,' he said. 'Enough, Nik.' I flung my boxer shorts (brick-red, navy trim) into his face, and stood in front of him naked from the waist down.

'You put them on!' I was shouting. 'Go on, *you* put them on!' I'm afraid these were my exact words. I could just make out, underneath my shorts, his look of horror. Then, wiping them from his face, he ran past me, and the front door slammed.

As a sequence of events it isn't much, God knows, but it felt like the end of everything, and I began to cry, not for Wills, but for myself. For the person I had been and for the person I was about to become.

Later that night I began to rage.


# IV

When I was a child I read about people who are

transformed into wolves or toads or bitter shrubs, and I was horrified. Was I frightened because I feared one day it would happen to me? Or did I secretly *want* to be transformed?

Suddenly, after that evening with Wills, nothing remained of what I had been: it was as if I had been turned into anti-matter, I wanted only to repudiate the life he and I had shared, to smash the house we had lived in together, to embezzle his money, slander him, dig up his garden, spit in his Evian. Memories of our life tormented me, insulted me, not necessarily the great moments but more often the little ones, mocking, insignificant details, the shape of his sleeping profile on the pillow, the old man's freckles across his back, the sound of his laughter, the peculiarities of his sexual parts. It was the greatest possible horror to be transformed in this way.

(What, I wonder now, does 'transformation' *mean*. Is it metamorphosis, or is it revelation? Perhaps it is catching sight of something in ourselves which we have never seen before. Like most people I thought I knew myself, and I was mistaken. I was altered, I was *deformed* by that alien rage which was apparently mine.)

For two days I went round our house, planning its destruction. How can I express the catastrophic desperation of this? The house had been our great shared love, our almost-consuming passion. We had decorated and redecorated, renovated and periodised and improved; we had been intensely domestic. Our preferred style was, dare I say it, *mousy*. Wills's favourite room was the conservatory, he would lie for hours on the settee covered in quilts, reading. Mine was the landing, I used to take books there and sprawl on the carpet, my nose next to the balustrades, or sit with my back against a wall and my knees up to my chest, trying to take in all the little angles made by the walls, the banisters, the doorways and the falling stairs, the bitty puzzle of light and solid.

All these rooms and spaces were lost to me now.

For two days I went round the house in a daze of affection, snooping like a voyeur, lovingly committing it to memory, and then, on the third, I went to town and bought five pounds of shelled prawns, four tubes of superglue, a pair of crimping shears, a packet of maximum thickness fuse wire, a large bag of mustard and watercress seeds, a sachet of industrial-strength glue powder, an economy-size tub of E45 cream, half a dozen live goldfish and a new shovel.

For three days fury lit me up like a drug; then, quite suddenly, I collapsed; between breakfast and lunch one Friday my anger entirely dissipated and I subsided into self-pity and sadness.

## V

I like to think that I did at least one useful thing. I like to think I learned what it is like to die. To all intents and purposes I *was* dying; like a dying man

I had already taken leave of the house, and now I went out into the neighbourhood to see it for the last time.

At odd times of the day, at five in the morning, or three in the afternoon when the schools emptied, or after midnight when the only sounds are the honks and huffings of birds on the lake, I found myself in the park or by the river – or simply in the street, lost in looking at it, at the dull rust-coloured saw-toothed gables, the repetitious dazzle of car roofs, the packed row of lovely, squashed houses with their ugly crusts of restoration and modernisation. It was an Indian summer; September glowed. The softness of the air gave the illusion of softness to everything else, buildings, front gardens, dustbins and gasometers, carports, roads and cars. More curious still, it produced in me a feeling of déjà vu, as if in the exact same weather, at a very particular time in the past, I had done something momentous which, like a vaguely sensed dream, I couldn't quite remember. For all these reasons my walks round Parkside seemed like a final reprise. As I went I thought that I would never again see the crocuses in the park or watch people playing tennis on the courts, never see the water-meadows flood in February or watch the inky shadows of the cypresses stretch across the brown summer grass towards the putting course, never see such things at all, never live again.

Walking home very sadly one evening I met Hilary Benedict who was telling Ben off for letting go of his balloon. It floated above us, moving more swiftly than you might imagine, rushing over the rooftops and trees until it was a silver thread against the deepening blue. Ben put his arms and wet face up to me and I lifted him.

'How easily we lose things,' I said. That's exactly what I said, I couldn't help it, and they looked at me.

Always, in the end, I was driven indoors, and sometimes Wills was there, sometimes not. But we never ate together and rarely spoke.

In fact he seemed to me more and more of an incredible figure: unreal. I had stopped questioning him and he had stopped acknowledging me. In front of him I was demure and tearful, perhaps I thought he might take pity and forgive me for whatever I had done – but he had taken on a lodger to move in at the end of the week. Whenever we coincided in the house I stopped and watched him with a sort of corrupted fascination. Where I had snooped before into empty rooms, now I snooped to catch glimpses of him. Not for consolation – consolation is the twist of the knife – but because I could not take my eyes off him. Once I stood in the doorway of the study for half an hour watching him scribble in a grey official-looking notebook. His head was bent towards me and I was shocked to see that he was going bald. This tiny detail seemed to make him altogether strange; I stared in horror at his thin bowed shoulders, his long, stockinged feet, his yellow fingers as if seeing them for the first time. He coughed mournfully, and scratched his legs, and I was mesmerised. For half an hour I watched him, whoever he was, and then I fled – whoever *I* was.

Every morning he cycled to the university precinct as usual. But I couldn't even get up, I lay in bed for hours, sometimes crying, sometimes wanking in that sad half-hearted way you do when what you are looking for is not an erotic thrill but the lost knack of something just out of reach, some sort of happiness, or at any rate a time-killing distraction. I began to feel that I might not make it to the end of the month without breaking down completely, and one morning I was so sad and lonely I telephoned Wills at work. I actually did that. Finally, he was the only person I had to talk to.

The receptionist put me through to his secretary who told me he was not available.

'I have his mobile number,' I said. 'I'll try that.'

'Mr Fleish is on long-term leave,' she said. Those are the words she used. Her voice was prim and snooty, conjuring up just-so blouses and spectacles, but there was a faint tone of embarrassment as well. After a silence which neither of us seemed to want to break I said, 'How long has he been on leave?'

'A fortnight. Would you like to speak to his assistant?'

I rang off and sat for a long time on the bed, with the phone in my hand. I remember looking round the room as if someone might be hiding by the wardrobe. I was frightened; the snooty receptionist had frightened me. Was it my sadness, or was it paranoia? Suddenly I began to believe in a conspiracy

— a conspiracy against *me*, of which Wills's inexplicable antipathy was only the tiniest part.

## VI

Conspiracies have the virtue of *explaining* things. I knew Wills was getting rid of me. Now I concluded that his reasons were malicious or judgemental.

Early the next morning I went to the park and sat on one of those stone slabs by the lake that look as if they have been excavated from a now-demolished stately building, and tried to think. I stared across the water. Its colour was always changing, and it contained all colours, all emotions, I had seen it run through sadness, happiness, hopefulness, desolation. But on that morning, in that hot and exhausted September, it was golden: the colour, I thought, of tranquillity.

Lulled by the weather I fell asleep, and had a disconcerting erotic dream from which I awoke with a fart as a pregnant woman was going past with a blindish terrier on a lead. It came to me that unless I talked to someone I would go mad, and with a start I realised that I had not spoken to anyone at all since Wills had told me to leave. Getting up stiffly from my ornamental slab, I went immediately to the house of a friend which overlooks the north side of the park.

We sat in his second-floor living room looking out over the lake and trees – yellow willows, bitter green

240

cypresses – listening to the tiny argumentative noises of coots and mallards, the view suddenly and oddly elongated and recessive. Already I felt it had been a mistake to come. Something was wrong. My friend kept looking round the room nervously as if expecting someone to walk in, and I heard myself as I talked, heard the precise tone, as if I were someone else with a different voice and different feelings.

'Do you remember that time,' I asked, 'when we discovered Wills had been having lessons in disco-dancing?'

His eyes betrayed his confusion. He has a little moustache he chews when he is nervous which makes him look demented.

'It's worse,' I said.

He seemed to both nod and shake his head, and abruptly rose to make more coffee.

'I'm worried about him,' I called after him, and he hummed under his breath in some non-committal way, and at that moment I realised that he knew exactly what Wills was doing, and would never tell me. I was furious. Getting up and preparing to leave, I stood at the window with the park below me hoping I wouldn't cry. Something had happened which was so massive and near I couldn't bring it into focus; though no one would explain, they all knew. *It was the conspiracy*.

'I wouldn't worry about Wills,' my friend called from the kitchen after a few minutes. His voice was shaky. 'He's absolutely fine. I'm sure he is.'

Something, some small tremor in my intestines

between my stomach and anus, went through me when I heard him say that, and I turned to face him as he came smiling through the kitchen door; and when he saw me looking at him his face fell.

# VII

The next day when Wills cycled off to work I followed, staying about fifty yards behind him and wearing a coat I hadn't worn in years. I did not run to a false moustache, though I considered it. There were dead leaves on the cycle path but the air was warm and the sky blue. Except for the fact that we were apart, we might have been setting off on one of our outings, to the Victoria over the river, or to the pick-your-own beyond the ring road.

How slowly Wills cycled, he seemed not just cautious but feeble, like an old man; it was hard to resist the temptation to overtake him. Slowly we went past the park, slowly along cramped streets lined with terrace cottages, slowly over the iron bridge at Nun's Wharf. Slowly we went across the main road and along the twisting cycle trail to the city centre, like two people intent on something other than their journey.

I was nauseous with excitement. I thought that with the discovery of where Wills had been going for the last fortnight I would expose the conspiracy and explain the change in him.

But he did not once deviate from his usual route to

work: we went – still slowly – through the shopping centre, past the theatre and the museum, into the university precincts, and when we reached the area shared by the science departments and the infirmary, he slowed, and I stopped. He went past the modernist tower block and across the face of the low-rise laboratories. I followed for a little distance, then hid behind a telephone box. I couldn't understand it: he was going to his office. A few seconds later he walked the length of the last link in the chain of offices, parked his bike outside, and went into the Department of Environmental Sciences where the Disasters Studies programme was based.

While students and academics and mothers with buggies went by I stood next to the telephone box, feeling that the conspiracy, far from being exposed, had deepened to the point where *even I seemed implicated*. Finally there was nothing for me to cling to. All my suspicions were unfounded. I had begun to turn away when I saw Wills come back out of the college entrance, and I froze. He crossed the road (so slowly, with a suddenly *suspicious* slowness), went a little way along the pavement, and turned into the infirmary.

The infirmary. It was as simple as that.

How long did I stay there on the street, holding onto my bicycle and looking as if I were queuing to use the telephone which I suppose remained unoccupied? Was it ten minutes, or half an hour, or all morning? There *was* a period, I remember, in which I beat the side of the telephone box with my hands, shouting, as if my sheer rage could propel me backwards in time away from everything, but I couldn't say how long it lasted. Then I was in our garden at home. I had not stopped crying. Do I dare admit that there was relief in the realisation that Wills still loved me?

# VIII

On the last day of September, my last day in the house, I cooked salmon en croûte, and at around eight, with the air still warm and the sunset sliding into darkness, we sat in the kitchen with a single candle on the table, and a Bach partita on the stereo in the living room like old times, the whole subject of my leaving lying unspoken between us. Though he had seen my bags packed at the top of the stairs Wills hadn't even asked where I was going. He pushed his salmon to the side of his plate and ate a slice of pear and sipped his fizzy water. We had been silent for a long time.

The Bach plotted its way towards a perfect conclusion.

We were both drinking water.

'Who's going to look after you?' I asked. He looked at me for a moment, and mumbled something about looking after himself before he met me.

'I mean, who's going to give you your injections when you can't manage it yourself?'

He sat quite still with his arm up, elbow crooked, and a piece of pear on a knife halfway to his mouth. I don't know why, but it's the pear I remember, sitting on the blade of his knife, glistening.

'I mean, who's going to pick you up when you fall and can't get up yourself? Who's going to change the sheets when you wet the bed?'

The pear slowly slid onto the tablecloth with a soft wet noise.

'Well?' I said.

'A nurse,' he said quietly.

There was a long pause in which we didn't hear the Bach.

'You *silly* fag,' I said.

That's all it took, in the end. That's all that was said. There was no need for either of us to mention love or fidelity or anything like that.

Now we both spend a lot of time lying awake at night. We think our own thoughts. Mostly I am struck by the immediate things, the way they exist so close to me, the quiet house at night, the shapes of things in the room, the sound of our breathing. Wills has changed. You wouldn't recognise him. I don't think of that. Sometimes I think of the prawns sewn into the curtains; of Wills's evening dress suits hanging in his wardrobe with the crotches cut out of them with a pair of crimping shears; of the address book and all the spare keys to the house buried in five separate holes in the rose bed; of the glue sachets fastened to the insides of the taps; of the goldfish dying in the cold water tank; of the mustard and cress sown into the guest room carpet; of the E45 cream in all the pots of Wills's live yoghurts in the fridge; of the super-thickness fuse wires in the fuse box under the stairs; of the pages of Wills's favourite books superglued together. But it doesn't matter if the house falls around us. We're lying here together, in the dark, motionless but changing, changing all the time, like parts of a chrysalis. At the bottom we are not ourselves, we never were, there were no changes, there was nothing but change. I don't think of it; it doesn't matter, it doesn't matter at all. We are lying here in the dark, thinking our own thoughts, and it's enough.